Carly combed her fingers through her hair. "Look, I, I, shouldn't have bothered you. It was stupid of me. I don't really know what —"

"Now, hold on," Lela said, torn. She felt a knot of remorse twist in her gut. Carly was a good kid, a smart kid, a kid who deserved to be supported, who deserved better than what Lela was willing to offer. But the fact was, Lela had no interest in getting involved with the students' lives. She was teaching high school only while she was finishing up her dissertation. Then she was off to a university. Anywhere. Far away was better. Safe in the front of the room with the backing of school policy not to interact with her constituents: the students. She wasn't about to start buying the kids Cokes and spending hours in a diner saving them from whatever domestic disasters they got into these days. And yet . . . what if Carly were really in some kind of trouble?

Carly grabbed her knapsack. "I should go."

"Wait," Lela said, and as soon as the word was out of her mouth, she felt her heart start to pound. The scream of the train whistle began in her head, and her body registered the shimmy of the tracks as the train drew nearer. *"Where are you going? Stay with me!"* the ghost-voice cried out. The rumbling and the whistling were so loud, she cowered. The air seemed magnetized, drawing her more powerfully each second. *"You promised! Come baaaaack!"*

"Ms. Johns? Ms. Johns, are you okay?"

LOOKING FOR NAIAD?

Buy our books at
www.naiadpress.com

or call our toll-free number
1-800-533-1973

or by fax (24 hours a day)
1-850-539-9731

One of our Own

A Novel by

Diane Salvatore

THE NAIAD PRESS, INC.
1999

Printed in the United States of America on acid-free paper
First Edition

Editor: Christine Cassidy
Cover designer: Bonnie Liss (Phoenix Graphics)
Typesetter: Sandi Stancil

Library of Congress Cataloging-in-Publication Data

Salvatore, Diane
    One of our own / by Diane Salvatore.
        p.   cm.
    ISBN 1-56280-243-7   (alk. paper)
    I. Title.
PS3569.A46234053   1999
813'.54—dc21
                                                           98-48244
                                                               CIP

About the Author

Diane Salvatore's first novel, *Benediction*, was a finalist for a Lambda Literary Award in 1991. She lives in New Jersey with her partner of seventeen years and their Cocker Spaniel.

Books by Diane Salvatore

Benediction

Love Zena Beth

Not Telling Mother

Paxton Court

One of Our Own

Come heart, fasten your armor
— Medea

Part I

...1

Jim Fallon loved his office hours with the kids. He considered it the best part of teaching, a chance to see his students up close, the way they really were, not the way they performed in front of their peers. Years ago he had stopped being surprised by the obnoxious classroom jokers who turned out to be secret scholars; this type was almost always a boy. Or the studious ones he'd thought couldn't even get a date who showed up, their hands shaking, wanting to know how their girlfriends could get abortions. It was true that it was mostly the boys who approached him with personal stuff, although once a female student had come to his office to make a clumsy pass. He hadn't been tempted at all; in fact, it was all he could do not to laugh.

Of course, that was a lot of years ago; he had been married then. Maybe now the joke was on him, since he was no longer young and boyish. These days he was indisputably middle-aged. His hair had thinned and his waist had thickened. He had grown a beard to compensate for his encroaching baldness, but he could think of nothing to do to camouflage his waistline. He imagined he seemed to the kids like part of the school furniture, like the trophy cases or the big marble science lab desks. He was purely functional, without mystery or controversy, without the intrigue necessary to hold an adolescent's imagination.

He was shoving all his papers into his canvas backpack when Lela Johns, his office mate and fellow English teacher, came in and fell into her chair at the other desk. She was, as usual, right on time for the office hours they were required to log with students. "Hey, Jim," she said. "Heading out?"

"And I can tell you'll be sorry to see me go," he said, mock-wounded. He liked Lela, despite her outrageously transparent effort to be unlikable. This was her very first teaching gig — that's how fresh out of grad school she was — and he wouldn't have minded being a mentor of sorts, but she had frozen him out enough times that he had mostly stopped trying. He kept holding out hope for at least cordial banter between them, and he admitted to himself that this hope was partly because she was so good-looking: glossy dark hair, often pulled back into a ponytail with a soft velvet scrunchie; dark, lushly lashed eyes; that intense, humorless manner that had made a romantic imprint on him during his own grad-school days when he had first fallen in love.

"Actually," Lela said, "I'd love it if you could stay instead of me. I'm not good at these requests to 'discuss personal problems.' "

He heard the reproach when she said "personal," as if the range of possible meanings ran from "ridiculous" to

4

"disgusting." She'd turned herself into the best kind of bait, though, because her very remoteness made her magnetic to the kids. He could see it when they were around her. The only reason the boys weren't lining up outside her door with lame excuses to talk about books or assignments was that Lela could be terrifying in the way she made it clear that they were all less interesting to her than the material, instead of the other way around. To the boys in particular this was a shock — and coming from an attractive woman, it was a direct hit. The girls were more inclined to agree with Lela's ordering of the world, so their teacher's stance probably seemed unremarkable, even appropriate. Whatever student it was who had decided that Lela Johns was a good shoulder to lean on had to be either particularly unconscious or particularly desperate.

"Who's the student?" Jim asked, on his feet, buttoning his jacket.

Lela swiveled around in her chair to face him. "Carly Matson."

The blush spread up his neck, warming his earlobes. "Oh, sure. Good student, good kid. Had her last year for Comp Two. God, hope it's nothing serious."

But he saw that Lela had spotted it, saw it register on her face in the form of slightly pursed lips, the unwavering gaze. She wouldn't ask, though; it wasn't Lela's style to ask for what wasn't offered.

"Well, every problem has a solution, right?" she said. "That's the Franklin High way, isn't it?"

"Do you want me to stay? I'm happy to, if you think I can help." He hoped his voice sounded normal, given that it felt like his tongue was sticking to the roof of his mouth. She swiveled away, waved him off. "Seriously," he said. "You know, I could just hang around, and if it looks like she's happy to talk to both of us, I'll just keep hanging around."

"And if she's not — happy to talk, that is?" Lela asked.

"Then I'll be outta here."

5

She was torn, he could tell. She rubbed a spot behind her ear.

"What time is she supposed to come?" he asked, stepping out into the hallway just as Carly was turning the hallway's far corner. She came loping his way, head down, in cowboy boots and a purple pea-coat; her hair, a long mass of brown curls, bounced behind her. Between last year and this she had crossed the divide between girl and young woman. She looked up suddenly, and maneuvered past him as if he were a telephone pole or a snow bank, remembering her manners, apparently, only at the last moment, mumbling "Hi, Mr. Fallon," when she was already across the threshold and in his office.

"Hi, Carly," he said. "I just got here," he said, unbuttoning his jacket. "I didn't realize Ms. Johns would be here, too." He knew that Lela was scowling at him, and he wouldn't meet her eyes. He felt suddenly clammy with possessiveness. He wasn't about to entrust Carly to Lela alone, Lela who had nothing at stake, no reason to care about this kid, not the way her mother cared, or even the way he cared. Why were teenagers perverse like that — throwing themselves at people who didn't give a shit?

Carly looked stricken, but he didn't let that stop him. He went over to his desk, unpacked the bag he had just packed.

"Oh, well, I made an appointment —" Carly began. She was twirling one of the buttons of her pea coat until, he was sure, it was just seconds away from coming free and clattering to the floor.

"Jim, I need the room," Lela said. "Actually."

He met her gaze. *I was doing you a favor.*

"We can go somewhere else, Carly," Lela said, getting up abruptly.

"No, no, look — I'm sorry. I, uh, should have called ahead. I'll clear out." His neck burned with a blush, and he got quickly packed and buttoned up again. "Well, I hope you're doing well, Carly. It's always nice to see you." What he wanted to do was lightly kiss her forehead and tell her he would protect her always. Instead, he clapped her shoulder roughly, as if they were rugby team mates, and walked out.

He got only a few paces down the hall when he heard the door click shut. He turned to look, knowing it would not open again.

It would not have been Lela's choice to have the office door shut; it just made the windowless room with its white, unadorned walls feel even more tomblike. She watched as Carly Matson slid her knapsack under the gray, plastic chair against the wall, moving carefully, as if the room were rigged with booby traps.

"Thanks for seeing me," Carly said.

Lela shrugged and slumped in her swivel chair, feigning casualness, hoping to get Carly to relax. Otherwise, they could be here for hours while the girl worked up the nerve to say whatever it was she had come to say. Carly, with her full sweep of wavy brown hair and dark, serious eyes, was only a few degrees away from full-blown womanhood. It was the age of limbo, when you were old enough to register your desires, yet young enough to botch everything badly if you acted on them. Lela did not envy her students their youth.

"I'm really enjoying your class," Carly said.

"I thought this wasn't about English." Lela meant it as a prod, but she saw on Carly's face that it had landed as a rebuke; she was fumbling this already. The girl lowered her eyes, hunched her shoulders a notch. Lela didn't want to be bruising, but neither did she want to play twenty questions.

"It's not. But I don't just enjoy your class because of, you know, English. I mean, I admire . . . you. A bunch of us do. We feel like we can talk to you."

Lela seized a pen and began to tap it on her knee. "Well, I've done absolutely nothing admirable, I'm afraid, and I don't really know that I'm the talking-to type. You're one of the best minds in my class, no question, but my area of expertise is pretty limited to that kind of evaluation. Wouldn't you feel more comfortable talking to one of the counselors?"

"I've *tried*," Carly said, pushing her hair behind one ear. "Mrs. Malloy. It was hopeless. *Completely* hopeless. I mean, she didn't say what I — she was just totally not ready for me. I can't go back there. Don't make me go back to her."

Lela straightened up. Rose Malloy was one of her least favorite people at the school. Parochial, righteous. She hated to think of her inflicting herself on Carly.

"Well, isn't there another counselor, then?"

"I can't talk to Mr. Hernandez. Not at all."

"You'd rather talk to a woman?" Lela guessed.

Carly nodded moodily.

Lela clasped her hands together into a fist; so it was sex, then, God help her. She sighed. "I can't promise I can help. But why don't you just tell me what the problem is."

The girl leaned back in the chair, crossed, then uncrossed

her legs. She shook her hair out from behind her ear. Then she leaned forward abruptly and sent the cup of pens and pencils clattering to the floor.

"Oh, God, I'm sorry," she said, running around the side of the desk, collecting rolling pens.

"Carly, forget it. I'll get them later. Sit down. Stop it, really. Sit down and tell me already."

The girl shuffled back to the chair, still scanning the floor anxiously, putting some of the pens and pencils back in the upright cup with great deliberation. She began chewing her bottom lip. Lela kept silent, not trusting herself to keep the frustration out of her voice.

"It's, um, my parents. My mom, really. I mean, my parents aren't getting along. At *all*. They think I don't know it, my little brother and me. Plus, my mom is on my case all the time, so *we're* not getting along and . . . I just feel like I can't stand to be in the house sometimes. A lot of times. And, um, I'm worried it's going to start hurting my grades."

Lela folded her arms. Carly was lying, Lela was sure, but she didn't know about what or to what degree or, more to the point, why. But she couldn't just come right out and call her on it. There had to be a good reason why Carly was going in circles this way, avoiding whatever it was she really wanted to say.

"Well, your grades right now are stellar as always."

"I know. But it's getting harder. A lot of times, I have to go stay at my friend Fran Reilly's house, so I can clear my head." Carly blushed.

Fran Reilly. Lela's shoulders stiffened. The girl was in Lela's class, too: blond, bored . . . butch. Lela didn't like to judge superficially, but she had registered, in a kind of impassive inventory of her student population, that Fran was probably a lesbian. There had been no reason to dwell on that fact or on her, except that Fran was something of a classroom disruption. She was volatile and charismatic, always muttering sarcastic asides Lela couldn't hear but that broke the kids up. They seemed in awe of her and vied for her attention. Lela wouldn't have guessed at the friendship between these two, though. What could it mean that Carly was going out of her way to mention it now? A spray of goose bumps ran up Lela's arms, and she felt the press of the room's stuffiness. She would not take the bait, would not pick up that particular conversational thread. She stuck to more conventional territory.

"So . . . you're here to let me know that your grades *might* drop?" Lela asked.

Carly combed her fingers through her hair. "Maybe. I mean, I guess, yes, but what I really wanted —" She stood up abruptly. "Look, I, I shouldn't have bothered you. It was stupid of me. I don't really know what —"

"Now, hold on," Lela said, torn. She felt a knot of remorse twist in her gut. Carly was a good kid, a smart kid, a kid who deserved to be supported, who deserved better than what Lela was willing to offer. But the fact was, Lela had no interest in getting involved with the students' lives. She was teaching high school only while she was finishing up her dissertation. Then she was off to a university. Anywhere. Far away was better. Safe in the front of the room with the backing of school policy not to interact with her constituents: the students. She wasn't about to start buying the kids Cokes and spending hours in a diner saving them from whatever domestic disasters they got into these days. And yet . . . what if Carly were really in some kind of trouble?

Carly grabbed her knapsack. "I should go."

"Wait," Lela said, and as soon as the word was out of her mouth, she felt her heart start to pound. The scream of the train whistle began in her head, and her body registered the shimmy of the tracks as the train drew nearer. *"Where are you going? Stay with me!"* the ghost-voice cried out. The rumbling and the whistling were so loud, she cowered. The air seemed magnetized, drawing her more powerfully each second. *"You promised! Come baaaaack!"*

"Ms. Johns? Ms. Johns, are you okay?"

Like a shutter closing over a camera eye, the scene

ended. But as short as it was, it left her back slightly damp, her legs weak as if after physical effort. When she realized what had happened — that she hadn't been able to sense the flashback coming — she felt panicky and couldn't meet Carly's eyes.

"Are you sick? Do you need a doctor?" Carly asked, her voice thin with fear.

"No, no. I'm okay," Lela said. "Just a little nausea. Maybe some bad milk in the cup of coffee I had before. And it's a little close in here." She got up and threw open the door. The small rush of air revived her some. "Maybe we should continue this another time."

"Yeah, sure." Carly kicked the chair leg in her scramble to get out. She paused at the door. "You're sure you don't want me to call anyone for you?"

"Not at all. It'll pass," Lela said, rolling her chair closer to the desk to hide her trembling legs.

Lela waited till she heard Carly's footsteps recede down the hallway before she closed the door again. Then she returned to her desk, buried her face in her arms and gave in to tears. "I'm sorry, I'm sorry, I'm sorry," she whispered, in a chant so low she could barely hear it herself.

...3

The phone rang only twice before Donna Matson picked it up. "Sweetheart, can you talk?" Jim said, not letting her finish "hello."

"Yes. Carly's not home yet —"

"I know, she's in my office, with my office mate. Evidently she had a personal problem to discuss and made an appointment."

"What kind of problem?" Donna asked, alarmed.

"Honey, I don't mean to scare you," Jim said. "I'm sure it's nothing. It was just . . . you haven't mentioned anything out of the ordinary. I wanted to know if everything was all right."

"Well, I'd be the last to know, you know that," Donna said, hating herself for sounding so self-pitying. "But I'll ask her when she comes home."

"You *can't*," Jim said sternly. "Not if you don't want to blow our cover. You'd have no way of knowing where she was unless Lela Johns or I told you directly."

"Who's Lela Johns?"

"My office mate. The teacher Carly's talking to at this moment. She's Carly's English teacher. She's new, young — just out of grad school. Still doing her dissertation. Hates teaching. Pretty nearly hates having to deal with the kids, as far as I can tell. Can't wait to get her degree and get the hell out."

The name rang a bell. Carly had mentioned a Ms. Johns a few times since the semester had begun in January, but she hadn't remembered what subject she taught. She'd found Carly experimenting with a scrunchie for her hair, an idea she'd gotten from this teacher. Donna had told her that her hair was too pretty to tie back. She felt a prickle of irritation. Who was this woman that Carly was so devoted to her opinion, more so than even her own mother's? "What kind of trouble could she be in?"

"Honey, it doesn't have to be trouble. She may just want to vent about something. Kids never talk to their parents, you know that. Look, why don't I come over, just for a little while? I've upset you."

Donna hesitated. They usually met in diners and little inns in the next town over. Sometimes he came to the house; it was fairly easy to get in and out during the day. Hugh was never home, and Jim would pull his car directly into the garage and enter the house from there, unseen, she was fairly certain. Automatic gargage doors had contributed significantly to the anonymity of the suburbs, she was sure, and New Jersey was no exception. As a result, she was not friendly enough with any of the neighbors that there was a risk of someone just dropping by. But right now, she was too

14

distracted to cope with him. "I'm afraid. She could come home any minute."

"I won't stay long," he said and hung up before she could refuse.

She had been the one to start their affair. When she thought about it now, it amazed her. She had called Jim at school last year, after one of her fights with Carly. He was Carly's English teacher, and she knew him by sight from some of the PTO meetings, enough to remember that he had seemed friendly and sympathetic. Not long into that first conversation, she had begun to cry and asked him if other mothers reported that their daughters hated them. His voice had been hypnotic: pleasantly deep and slow, like a deejay on a late-night jazz station. They met several times for a month before she realized she had been seduced; before that, she had really believed she'd just wanted a friend. And it was another month after that before she found herself shyly naked on cool sheets in what would become their regular place.

Even so, she had imagined that he was going to be a temporary lapse, a little hole in her marital fidelity that she'd patch up with Hugh later with regret and extra affection. But now that it had gone on more than a year with Jim, she knew it was a full-blown complication, weighed down with risks she had not planned on taking: people at school suspecting, getting pregnant (since she and Hugh didn't sleep together anymore), Hugh finding out and confronting her, which she still imagined he'd do because she did not think he had stopped caring for her completely.

In the meantime, Jim's affection was something she had gotten used to, like an extra blanket on a damp night. And though she hadn't been counting on this at all, he had proven to be an excellent lover. As in love with Hugh as she had been from the beginning of their marriage, sex between

15

them had always been procedural at best. Jim's lovemaking, by contrast, reminded her of archaeologists she'd seen in documentaries, kneeling for hours in the heat, their faces pressed close to rock, making patient brush strokes, blowing as lightly as you would on a sleeping baby, till a brand new shape emerged. But still, she couldn't picture Jim as her husband, the whole story, the main event. It was no reflection on him; it was just the circumstances. He had come into her life as an auxiliary, and the heart sometimes obeyed the strictest caste system.

She heard a rap at the back door; she saw Jim's bearded face, weirdly distorted through the small window of beveled glass.

"Hi," he said, taking her in his husky arms, getting ready, she sensed, to linger.

She broke away, took his coat, poured hot water over coffee bags for both of them.

"What could it be about?" she asked, picking up where they'd left off on the phone.

"I'm sorry I told you," he said. "It's not like she showed up at the local drug-abuse clinic. Or the Young Parents' group. Whatever it is, it can't be too terrible if she went to her English teacher about it."

But she knew from his tone that he was jealous Carly hadn't picked him. Carly, who he hoped might be his responsibility one day if Hugh were out of the way. She saw that he felt a father's pride in Carly's work at school, worried over her coming home late almost as much as she did. Sometimes she thought he wanted fatherhood as much as he wanted to be a husband again; he and his first wife had split before they'd had any kids.

"Do you think it's about a boy?" she asked. "Maybe she feels like she can't talk to me about that."

"I haven't seen her hanging out with any of the guys in particular. But I don't see her all the time, of course, and some- times not for days at a time."

"I can never get her to talk about boys at all. For a while,

Hugh and I —" she saw him flinch at the mention of his name — "were happy that she didn't seem boy-crazy, but now, well, I admit I'm a little worried. She gives me these cutting looks whenever I try to find out if she's interested in any boy in particular. Sometimes I think she knows about us — I mean, not you per se, but that there's someone. And she's punishing me with her silence."

"It's a hellish time, adolescence. If you can just hang on till she's about twenty-four, everything will be okay."

He meant to make her feel better with his jokes, but as she bobbed her coffee bag in her mug of hot water, she felt her mood darken. There was more on her mind than she would admit to Jim, or even to Hugh: that sometimes she worried that Carly wasn't interested in boys at all, that maybe she had taken some twisted lesson from the hostility in the house between her parents. Besides, she thought Carly was too stuck to this friend of hers, this Fran, whom Donna didn't like at all. There was something beyond tomboy about her. Donna often tried to think how to warn Carly that some girls were strange — maybe this girl — but she worried that it would make Carly angry, push her away even more, so she'd said nothing about it so far.

"You look like a lost soul. Come sit on my lap. I *crave* you."

"Jim, I'm a wreck —"

"A purely innocent request."

She obliged him, wrapping her arms around his neck and relaxing against him. It was this that she kept coming back for, his particular masculine strength, the promise of safety, however illusory.

"When can we be a family?" he whispered, his voice against her cheek, cajoling, like a child asking to stay up an hour longer.

She took his face in both hands, her fingers against his wiry beard. His eyes were wet. A quiver of fear shot from her stomach to the soles of her feet; not since her father cried at her mother's funeral ten years ago had she seen a man in

17

tears. She did not want to be powerful enough to provoke this.

"Don't do this to yourself, Jim," she said. "We're together, aren't we?"

"I just want to be there for the both of you, like you deserve," he said.

"You are," she said, knowing it was not what he meant.

Donna was going through the motions of cooking and watching TV, but she was really just was waiting for Carly to come through the door. She had been rehearsing, as she reread the orzo directions, how she could ask Carly about this appointment with a teacher she wasn't supposed to know about.

"Home, Mom," Carly said, already retreating down the hall to her room. Her tone was unremarkable, unrevealing.

"Hi," Donna sang out. Why she still bothered to muster vigorous cheerfulness was a mystery even to her. She knew it only annoyed Carly. She followed her daughter down the hall, carrying her dish towel, eager to get to her room before Carly shut the door, picked up the phone or turned on her stereo. "I'm making almond-crusted chicken breasts with orzo — how's that sound?"

"Complicated," Carly said, flinging her knapsack on the bed. "Got a lot of homework to do, Mom."

"What kind?" Donna said, defying Carly's force field of disapproval and sitting down on the bed anyway. Donna prided herself on having no illusions about the difficulty of parenting. You had to put your own ego aside constantly. You couldn't expect to be liked. You had to risk being hated. But sooner or later, if you'd done the right thing, your kids grew up to be adults who thanked and loved you. That's what she believed. "What kind?" Donna repeated.

Carly glared as if she'd been asked an inappropriately personal question. "English."

Oh, providence. A better opening Donna could not have hoped for. "English — I used to like that, too. What are you reading now?"

Carly was all small, jerky movements; Donna knew she was hot-wired with irritation. "Early twentieth century American writers."

"Good teacher?" Donna asked, nearly holding her breath.

"Okay."

"Is he cute? I always used to have crushes on my English teachers."

"Not a guy, Mom. A woman. She's very smart. I've told you about her before." Angry now. Proprietary. Smug. "Ms. Johns."

"Smart? In what way?" Donna asked casually. She got up, crossed the room to the window, feigned interest in a curling corner of wallpaper. She had promised Carly that when they were ready to redecorate, Carly would have a say about the wallpaper.

"I dunno, but I've got a lot reading to do now."

Donna regarded her daughter for a long moment. "In every way not like me, is what you mean."

"Mom, really, what is this?" Carly was at her desk now, yanking books out of her backpack.

"You never talk to me, is what. You're either at Fran's house, or you're locked in your room for hours on the phone. You're never at a loss for words with your friends. Why don't you ever talk to me? We used to talk, you know." *Oh God*, she was crying. She hadn't known the pain was so close to the surface. She flashed on a memory of herself with Carly, age six, playing tea party in this very room when the wallpaper was a butterfly pattern, and Carly would prattle on for hours about nothing, and then trail Donna down the hall to the kitchen where she had to get dinner ready, and say, "And you know what else, Mommy? You know what else?" just to keep her near.

"Mom, really." Carly looked up. Her face was cold; her face was her father's. "Get a grip."

Whatever extra measure of will it took, Donna didn't have it. She was on empty. There was nothing to do but give Carly what she wanted, to leave her alone, and to be left alone herself.

...4

Dear Diary:

Made a first-class ass of myself in Ms. Johns' office today. I can hardly even think about it without wanting to crawl under the bed and stay there for like a million years. How am I going to face her again in class? I knocked over the pencil holder and almost knocked over the chair — I mean, I was like Klutz Central! And then I was going on about my mother, as if!

I did manage to mention Fran's name, said we were friends and that I stayed over at her house. Ms. Johns got this look on her face like I said I did Satanic sacrifice on the weekends for fun and profit. Have no idea what to make of that. Either she doesn't think too much of Fran or she suspected the whole thing right away and she's totally creeped out.

The meeting got cut short though, because she had this weird episode while we were talking. Like she was going to hurl or something. Except it was more than that. She got this creepy transfixed look on her face, like she was in another world, and was muttering, almost. Then she snapped out of it just as fast and seemed really embarrassed. It scared me. I wonder if she's like, epileptic or something and doesn't want anyone to know.

So now I'm like back to square one. I don't know who to tell about me and Fran. I mean, if there still is a "me and Fran" after last week. When I even think about her kissing me, my stomach goes all fluttery, but then she can be so cruel, ignoring me in class and flirting with Melanie from gym class, right in front of me. (Melanie's clueless about what Fran is doing, but I know.)

I have no one to listen to me. I thought about going on the Web and finding a chat room but I just think: who ARE those people? Why would anyone want to talk to strangers, and disembodied strangers at that? I don't know why exactly I elected Ms. Johns to be my savior or something — I guess something about the way she seems so in control, and so smart. I admire that. And I've never had a teacher who really made me feel like the girls were just as important, maybe more important, than the boys. We had another young teacher last year and she half flirted with the boys most of the time.

I know it sounds crazy, but I wish Ms. Johns could be my friend or big sister. I feel like she would totally understand me and take me under her wing. I feel like I need a wing to be taken under. I can't do this alone! I'm going to have to find some other way to tell her. Even with as bad as it went today, something tells me not to give up hope. I mean, I think about the way she teaches. She _feels_ *the stories, you can tell. Sometimes she reads a passage aloud — we're doing Willa Cather now — and it's as if she makes the whole thing comes to life.*

I know Mom would say, Why can't you talk your family? Well, as if! Dad's mentally checked out, my brother is too little, and Mom just wants me to be a carbon copy of her.

And as for Fran — when she loves me I feel like the whole world is spinning right, but then she goes and acts like a jerk and it's the worst. Why does she do that? Who am I supposed to ask? Yeah, I have my regular girlfriends, but they are so into their boyfriends I can't imagine laying this on them. Besides, who would change next to me in gym anymore? I just want somebody who knows me to accept me, to tell me I'm not crazy, to tell me it'll get better. I just think, if I could get to be Ms. Johns' age, then everything would be all right. Then nobody could make me feel bad, nobody could tell me what to do.

...5

Lela swung by the teachers' lounge and pulled out the flyers and mail from the little wooden slot that had her name taped, slightly askew, underneath. There were repeat notices about due dates to submit grades, guidelines for the proper way to fill in the endless records they were required to keep, pleas for volunteers for this committee or that. After a cursory glance, she began pitching it, piece by piece, into a nearby trash pail. Then she heard someone laugh.

"Tending to departmental business, I see," Jim Fallon said, leaning against the wall, stirring a paper cup of coffee.

"Well, I . . ." she said, losing, by a beat, the moment in

which she might have said something clever in return. The fact was she didn't care enough about school business to be arch or contemptuous. This was not a career for her, the way it was for people like Jim. With any luck, she'd be out of here in a year — two at the most, God help her — and Franklin and all its inhabitants would be a verbal footnote during party conversation, not even worth the effort of anything beyond generic description. All the specifics — moments like this one when she was aware of the tan and black speckled tiles beneath her feet, the dust-and-varnish smell of the wall of in-boxes — would fade from memory.

"Have they started to turn the screws yet?" Jim asked. "I hear they're desperate for an assistant drama coach."

"I don't know the first thing about acting," Lela said, feeling penned in by Jim Fallon's hulking frame and unyielding gaze.

"The kids don't either — that's why it's a beautiful system."

She was aware of his increasingly acute interest in her. It didn't feel like sexual interest, but maybe that was just because he was awkward, a touch overeager. It was probably what the kids sensed in him, too, that he wanted, just a little too keenly, for them to confide in him, and that made them suspicious and tight-lipped.

"Well, with my dissertation, I haven't got time for anything extracurricular, which I told them when they hired me. Maybe that's why they've laid off me. Unless you've been chosen to relay the messages in what is to seem a less pressured way." She smiled weakly and excused herself to step around him and closer to the door.

"No, I come unarmed, an ambassador of no particular country. But you know, I could name more than a few teachers who are here ten, twelve years, who keep telling me this is only a temporary gig. Teaching has a way of growing on you. You might want to give it a chance. You'll see, before you know it, you'll be one of our own."

She studied him, trying to figure what he really wanted.

Maybe he took her stand-offish attitude — she knew she didn't do much to conceal it — as an affront to his own career choice. Or maybe he just saw all women as works in progress, perpetually open to advice and direction.

He seemed to take her pause as encouragement. "Want to grab a cup of coffee?" he asked. "They actually don't make a bad cup around the corner — better than this stuff I'm guzzling, anyway."

"I really can't today," she said.

"Say no more," he said. "Listen, tell me, though. How did it go with Carly Matson the other day? You survive?"

"Yeah, sure," she said, turning away so he wouldn't catch her frown. Was this his story, then? Did he hit on the girls, breathe a little too close to their necks when they came to see him in his office? It occurred to her now that he was only pretending to be interested in her; it was Carly he was intent on. Had he slipped a little tongue in her ear during some past visit and now he was sweating it, hoping Carly hadn't ratted on him? "No problem, actually," Lela said, studying his expression for some small betrayal of fear. But she saw nothing except mild disappointment.

"Good, then, you're getting the hang of it." He toasted her with his cup, reached into his own mail slot and waved good-bye with some papers.

Lela pushed through the front doors and stepped outside, feeling a mild hangover of regret. She had probably been too brusque; it wouldn't hurt her to have an ally or two at Franklin. Why did she have to go around sticking pins in people? But she knew why: it was a habit she'd developed under duress and been unable to break.

The sun on the parking lot leeched away color and made the cars look like gun metal, all sheen and glare. She rummaged in her bag for her keys as she walked, squinting down the rows till she found her burgundy Saturn. When she let herself in the car, she realized she still had most of the mail she meant to chuck out. She threw it on the passenger seat, and as it fanned out, she spotted an envelope she hadn't noticed before.

"*Personal and confidential*" was handwritten across the front. She held it for a few seconds, not breathing. Then she tore it open.

Dear Ms. Johns:

I'm sorry if I upset you the other day in your office. I think I blurted out a bunch of strange stuff that didn't make much sense. And that's because none of it was what I wanted to talk about.

Of course, what I actually wanted to talk about is pretty strange, too, I guess, but here goes.

There's a girl in my class, and we are going together, the way a guy and a girl do, I mean. There, I said it. I know you are probably shocked to hear this and of course I'm trusting you completely to keep this secret. I've been keeping it secret for six months now, and that's the problem. I've been wishing I could tell someone, just to talk about it, but I don't know who is safe. Things are not really going great with this girl and me, and I don't even know for sure if I am a lesbian. She says she is, and she has other friends we hang with who are, but I've been wanting to talk to someone I know, someone I respect.

I can't tell my parents, even though they always told me I could tell them anything. I don't think they meant <u>this</u>. I guess that was part of the reason my mother came up in our conversation. Because mostly I'm scared to death of her finding out and stopping me from seeing —

Here a word had been violently crossed out.

— this girl I think I am in love with. (Sometimes,

anyway. Other times she makes me so angry I hate her.)

Well, I don't really know where to go from here. I hope you won't think I'm a freak. I'm not exactly sure why I felt I could turn to you with this, in case you're wondering, but I just did.

Sincerely,
C. M.

The stale air in the car pressed in around Lela. She jerked the key in the ignition and turned the vent on high. Folding up the letter as small as she could, she stuffed it into her front pants pocket. She'd burn it in the sink when she got home. How crazy *was* this girl that she'd put such things in writing? Did she have any concept how it would look, what might happen, if it were found by someone else?

Lela pulled out of the lot. No more confessional letters — she was going to have to make *that* perfectly clear. No more confessions, period. Why did Carly think she could help? She couldn't, she'd proven that before. And why were people always closing in on her, making that demand? *Stay with me. You said we'd be together always,* the voice accused. *You'll never see me again if you don't come now. I'm doing it, I'm really going through with it, I'm not kidding, stay with me, you promised! You promised! Come back!*

"Hey, lady — watch where the hell you're going!" a screaming face said from the car passing in front of her. The light was red, and yet her car was a good ways into the intersection. Her heart was poundng in her throat, and she backed up the car slowly, by inches. This was new, and terrible: she'd never before had a flashback while driving. Her eyes welled with tears. It just wasn't fair. After ten years, they not only weren't getting better; it seemed they could still get worse.

Her hands trembled on the wheel as she waited for the

28

light to change. It was Carly's fault, she decided, as she drove the rest of the way as slowly as an eighty-year-old. Coming into Carly's orbit was triggering too many memories, stirring up too much history. It had to stop, cold. For both their sakes.

...6

Kit sat waiting at the table in the cozy, dimly lit restaurant. It was a terrific find, just the kind of place she was sure Lela would like — shiny copper pans hanging decoratively on the brick walls, sheer curtains tied back with velvet sashes. And it had a menu heavy on seafood and pasta, the only kind of fare Kit had ever seen Lela eat.

Kit had had plenty of time to study the menu, too, because Lela was so late. She should be used to it by now, Kit reflected, running her hand through her short, blond hair. Wait was all Lela ever made her do.

They had met four months ago at a party; Kit remembered the moment Lela entered the room. She'd had on jeans and a black Izod, the floppy collar turned up. Kit had felt Lela's image log on in her brain like one of those medical computers, where a person's body is translated into swirls of color, violet and cherry red, registering body heat and blood flow. Lela was there to be fixed up with the host's best friend. Kit had eavesdropped from the over-soft couch across from them, listening as Lela and her fix-up bombed together. At one point they had a ten-minute conversation about types of tea, before looking away from each other, defeated.

When Lela had gotten up and headed into the kitchen, Kit followed. "Blind dates are rough, huh?" Kit said. Lela arched one eyebrow; it was a small gesture, but Kit felt it acknowledged them as conspirators.

"I don't know why I let myself get talked into them," Lela said. "My friends all seem to think being single is a condition that needs curing."

Looking back, Kit couldn't say she hadn't been warned: Lela's first sentence to her had been a declaration of independence.

Later, as they were getting to know each other, Kit had been surprised to learn that Lela was a teacher. Lela didn't strike her as especially nurturing or even interested in imparting information. In fact, she had to be drawn out and avoided debate. If it looked as though they might disagree about something, even something as innocuous as the merits of a movie, she'd quietly withdraw, rigid with indifference. It was a major disappointment to Kit, since she herself enjoyed well-mannered sparring and insisted on knowing what people cared about. And Kit could see that Lela did care about things. It was maddening that she so rarely revealed what they were.

They were not lovers, not yet, as much as Kit wanted that. Meanwhile, Kit felt drenched with wanting Lela, completely submerged. But Lela maintained her tightly wrapped cool. She was not the relationship type, Lela kept saying, or other empty slogans that Kit couldn't reason away.

Kit did not like being on the wanting-more end of things, and she told herself she needed to pull back, be less invested, stay open to meeting other women. But her heart wasn't in it. She believed that, in time, Lela would be ready. She was prepared to be patient and steady and wait out whatever Lela's wariness was. Someone had probably hurt her — badly — and Kit was having to pay the penance. When she looked up and spotted Lela making her way to the table — her glossy black hair swinging loosely with her graceful step — she was reminded instantly why Lela was worth the wait.

After spending most of the meal carrying nearly the entire conversation, Kit finally gave up. "You're a million miles away. Mind telling me where?"

"Sorry," Lela said. "I guess I don't feel much like talking. Don't take it personally." Lela was toying with the edge of the wicker bread basket, giving it careful attention.

"I'm not supposed to take anything you do or say in my presence personally," Kit said, her cheeks warming with anger. "Well, you know what? You alone are not immune to the laws of physics. When you're with people, you need to take into consideration that you have an effect on them, and vice versa. I can take it if you tell me I bore you. I'd just like to have some effect, of any goddamn kind."

Lela studied her plate. "I'm not bored," she said. "You're not boring. It's not boredom." A tiny piece of the wicker snapped off between Lela's fingers.

"Shall we conjugate further?" Kit said, and then instantly regretted the sarcasm. She didn't want to be a bully. "What is it, then?" she asked, softening.

Lela shrugged. "I told you. I'm just in a quiet mood."

Kit leaned back in her chair, shaken to find herself close to tears. "I'm way out here, you know, on a limb. Because I'm in love with you," she finished in a whisper.

Lela shut her eyes. "Don't be, please."

Kit wasn't sure she heard right. "*Don't* be? It's not exactly optional. You don't get to *decide*, based on whether it's convenient." She tried to compose herself, watching as Lela continued to avoid her eyes and now turned to aligning her utensils. She was hunched defensively, like a suspect in a police interrogation. "Look," Kit said, "it's okay if you don't feel the same way. In fact, I know you don't. I don't need you to." Two out of three of these were lies.

A busboy briskly cleared their plates away. "Okay, look," Lela said after he'd gone. She unbuttoned the sleeves of her white Oxford shirt and rolled them back. "A student just left me a confidential note in my mailbox, telling me, basically, that she's having an affair with another girl at school and asking if I could help her figure out if she's really a lesbian."

This was certainly not what Kit was expecting, but it was perhaps the most intimate thing Lela had ever told her. The note had obviously hit a nerve, and that in itself wasn't surprising: Lela was as closeted as they get. Kit's friends had warned her this was bad news for any romance. A lesbian in the closet, they told her, would always slam the door shut whenever she felt threatened — and she'd be on the other side of it, alone. "That's pretty intense," Kit said, carefully. "What are you going to do?"

"*Do?* What should I be expected to do? I burned the letter in the sink right before I came to meet you. Doesn't this girl have a clue how much trouble she could get me into? I can't have it getting around that I'm sympathetic to —" she lowered her voice — "lesbian causes."

"Hey, you don't have to defend yourself to me," Kit said.

"But I *do* have to defend myself. Why should I risk my career on this girl? There are other places she can turn. There isn't a single thing I can do for her."

Kit heard the strain in Lela's voice, and she guessed that

she was trying to convince herself as much as anyone else. She sensed that Lela badly wanted to help the girl but was afraid. But of what? Whoever the girl was, Kit already felt a bond with her. They had some- thing in common, after all: wanting Lela's affection and attention. "You know, it had to be hard as hell for this girl to come to you."

"Well, why *is* she coming to me? Do I — do I look . . . *obvious*?" Lela was yanking her hair behind one ear.

"Well, *I* don't think so," Kit said. "Besides, maybe she hasn't given a thought at all to whether you're a lesbian. It could just be that she likes you or looks up to you. That wouldn't be so far-fetched." Kit smiled, imaging how Lela must seem to her students — glamorous and remote. "Or it could be that the kid's got gaydar."

"How could that *be*? I stick strictly to the text. I don't waver from it. I never talk about myself or venture an opinion."

"God, Lela, where did you get the idea that it's a crime to reveal your personality?"

"Where? I'll tell you *exactly* where. It's in black and white, in the policy the school board adopted last year. Teachers aren't allowed to state even straightforward facts about homosexuality or make any mention of it, in classes or in clubs — whether it's sex ed or social studies or English or the debate team. And forget it if you or a counselor are judged to have made any remarks to a student that could be construed as actually *encouraging* or supportive of homosexuality. And that includes everything right down to 'Honey, you *can* have a nice life with another woman. Now take that shotgun out of your mouth.' And it could even include not being able to reprimand a kid for saying, 'God made AIDS to kill fags.' I *might* be able to defend myself for telling a kid not to wish another human would be killed, but I'm not allowed to say why fags *in particular* should be able to live in peace, or why gay men aren't the only ones to die of AIDS."

Kit felt harpooned to the chair. She had never heard Lela

speak with such passion, and she hadn't realized this was going on at Franklin. She wasn't a parent, wasn't part of the lesbian baby boom, so she didn't pay much attention to school issues. But this was hair-raising stuff. "And you signed on for that? Who's going to fight this stuff if people like you don't?"

"Oh, people like *me*? How about people like *you*, a self-employed graphic designer who can afford to have politically correct opinions about teachers because you don't have to make a living as one?"

"But that's ridiculous," Kit said, trying not to stammer with rage. "Why would the school system listen to an outsider like me on the subject of gay teachers?"

"And why in God's name would they listen to a gay teacher?"

Kit sat back, reeling over how quickly they'd gotten into this ugly fight. She catalogued the things Lela had just accused her of being: a dilettante, a hypocrite, an apathetic, self-involved bystander. Was this really how Lela saw her? She stole a glance at Lela as she was rubbing her temples and decided to stay away from the personal implications until they both had their equilibrium back. For now, it seemed safer to rail on about social policy.

"How are they getting away with this?" Kit asked. "It sounds illegal to me. I didn't think New Jersey was the backwoods or anything."

"The right is deliberately doing grass-roots initiatives. They play just below the national news radar, so they make a lot of progress without attracting a lot of attention. Besides, people don't realize how much power local governments and school boards really have. Unless someone were policing a million different municipalities all the time, they can get away with all kinds of stuff if the majority is in favor."

"It's amazing to me," Kit said. "Twenty years ago, gays and lesbians played silently by the rules. Now school boards have to write it all down and remind us. I guess that's some kind of progress."

"It doesn't feel like progress from where I'm sitting."

Kit was beginning to feel defeated. She didn't seem to be able to say a single thing that Lela didn't attack. But then a new thought occurred to her. What better place for a closeted lesbian to work than some place where she was bound by contract to stay put in that very closet? Maybe Lela had, without fully realizing it, picked a setting where she didn't have to debate whether to come out, where she could blame the powers that be for deciding for her. And maybe this student had unwittingly made Lela confront her own hypocrisy and cowardice. "You know," Kit said, "I think what's making you crazy is that you really want to help this girl."

"*Don't tell me what I'm thinking,*" Lela said, her voice steely.

"Hey, I'm sorry." Kit realized all at once she had no experience with Lela's real emotions. She felt on land mines. "I thought maybe we could figure out something you could do or say to her to help. The world is supposedly more liberal, but it's still tough for gay teenagers — the suicide rate is still higher for gay kids than straight."

Kit fell silent as she watched the coffee cup in Lela's hand start to shake, first slightly, then violently, as if Lela alone, in the whole restaurant, were sitting on a tremor. Her complexion turned chalky, her lips parted in a pant. The cup then fell with a clatter, shooting coffee across the stark white table and attracting the glances of nearby diners. Lela pushed away from the table and broke into a trot, headed for the door.

"Lela, wait!" Kit called out, frantic. *What the hell was going on?* She yanked her wallet out of her back pocket, threw some bills onto the table and raced for the door.

But by the time she got to the parking lot, Lela's car was already gone.

...7

Two English classes had gone by since Lela found Carly's note in her box, and she had not exchanged a word with the girl yet, either during or after class. Every time the kids filed out, Lela braced herself for Carly to linger. She could feel the weight of Carly's expectation, like a physical force, and she resented being put in the position of withholding something she had never offered.

It also hadn't escaped Lela's notice that Carly had started sitting next to Fran Reilly in class — Fran with her flat, blank, pale face, her blond hair combed forward like a woodpecker's plume. Lela assumed Fran was the name Carly had crossed out in the letter, since hers was the name Carly had mentioned when she'd come to Lela's office.

Lela headed slowly down the school corridors and out into the parking lot. She'd felt heavy-hearted and fatigued since getting Carly's note, and she regretted telling Kit about it. She kept hearing her say, *What are you going to do?* and then her own answer — *nothing, nothing, nothing* — and seeing the look of shocked disapproval wash over Kit's face. It hurt — Kit had no idea how much — but neither Carly nor Kit had any right to put this responsibility on her. No one knew what she was feeling. She couldn't expect anyone to understand.

Lela unlocked her car door and was about to slip into the front seat when she spotted two girls on the grassy island across the lot, leaning like bookends against a tree. She fished out her glasses, which she wore only to drive. They were part of the devil's bargain she'd made with her computer, the toll exacted for all those hours as a grad student hunkered too near the screen.

The two girls, she saw now, were Carly and Fran. Her neck burned with self-consciousness. Were they waiting for her, having figured out which car was hers? Were they flaunting their affair in front of her, hoping she'd slip up and reveal herself somehow? She was not going to let this drag on any longer. She shouted across the lot. "Carly? Carly, is that you?"

Carly stirred, stood away from the tree, then turned to Fran and said something that made her stalk away. Carly stooped to pick up her backpack and headed slowly over.

"Hi, Ms. Johns." She held a hand over her eyes like a visor.

"Hi. Look —"

"You know, I want to apologize for the note I left you," Carly interrupted. "I was out of line. I put you on the spot. And I wanted you to know I'm okay now, I'm not worried, I mean, there's nothing to worry *about* and I don't want you to worry, is what I mean." Carly was squinting hard, having placed herself directly in the sun's path.

Lela was unprepared for the change in tactics. "Ah," she said, patting the roof of her car, trying to organize her feelings — disappointment and disbelief chief among them. No doubt her stupid, graceless performance the other day in her office — plus stonewalling on the note — had ranked her up there, in Carly's mind, with the likes of the obtuse counselor Mrs. Malloy. She ought to be happy, Lela reminded herself, since she had been trying hard to be considered irrelevant. "Ah," she said again.

Carly swung her backpack to her other shoulder, nervous, Lela could see, waiting to be dismissed.

"Look, I know I told you I couldn't help," Lela began. "And I can't, that's true. But I did go ahead and look into some things for you." She stepped back from the open car door so that Carly could angle away from the glare. "There's a group, in Manhattan — it's called Gay Youth. Here's the phone number," she said, quickly handing over the piece of paper she had been carrying around. "But, uh, this is an unofficial recommendation. After this moment, I've never heard of it in my life. Do you understand?"

Carly let her backpack slide off her shoulder and dangle at her knee, as if she'd suddenly been drained of energy. She held Lela's eyes for a beat, then looked down at the piece of paper. "Sure, thanks, I —"

"Don't mention it. Literally," Lela said, swinging down into the driver's seat, but not before registering Fran's figure, across the way, still and watchful. Just what she needed, some jealous baby butch nursing a grudge. She pulled the door shut, and Carly stepped back. Lela's heart had pushed its way into her throat; she couldn't have felt more reckless had she been jumping from rooftops. Carly leaned down just as Lela turned the key in the ignition. Carly was about to say something more, but Lela simply waved, backed the car out and drove off.

...8

They were lying in Donna's bed, side by side, the sheets covering them as chastely as an old married couple. Donna always liked to be quiet afterwards, which frustrated Jim, because it was then that his own thoughts were racing.

He scanned the room. Donna was always careful not to leave any signs of Hugh around — never an overlooked bottle of after-shave on his night table, or folded socks waiting to be stashed in his bureau drawer. But there didn't have to be. Jim sensed him everywhere in the room, the room he had nearly memorized, with its rosebud wallpaper and silver-rose carpet, its glossy, dark wood dressers. Hugh was the one with the right to come and go here, and the fact that he didn't love Donna didn't make Jim feel any less like a trespasser.

The hiding took its toll on him, made him suspicious and hyper-vigilant. He worried about everything. He had begun to suspect that Donna was faking in bed. He wasn't doing anything differently, but he could sense her distraction. He had started to work out at a gym, but she didn't seem to notice. He continued to hate that she would never meet him at his place, where they could have real privacy without fear of discovery, and although he had started to push this point hard, she continued to coolly refuse. She seemed to simply find it more convenient to be in her own house, where she didn't have to schedule additional drive time back and forth, or invent places to say she'd supposedly gone.

He rolled onto his side. "I want to be able to take you places, go out to dinner, go on a Caribbean vacation. I hate living this way."

"Shhhh," she said. "So greedy." She smiled at him lazily. "You were amazing just now."

He fell onto his back. The compliment disarmed him, as she probably calculated that it would, but he felt manipulated. He didn't want to be some stud; he wanted to be her husband. "He's away more than he's home."

"Which is how we can afford to be together so often."

"We could be together all the time," he said. "Unless that's what you don't want. Maybe that's why I'm getting nowhere on this point."

She got up, slipped into a robe. "What is it with men? You all think if you just keep insisting on something, something *you* want, eventually a woman will realize she didn't mean no, after all."

He sat up. "Is that what you think? I'm just trying to make it add up. If you say you love me and not him —"

"Just because sometimes I hate Hugh doesn't mean I don't still love him most of the time."

He stared at her, watching her pull the waist sash on her robe into a tight knot. "So what am I supposed to do? Hope that you grow to hate him more often than not?"

"Why not? I do. All the time."

He needed to stop talking this out with her. His friends said so. He needed to start being less available, let her see what it felt like to be kept hanging. But he didn't know how to pretend to feel something he didn't, or how not to feel something that he did.

Jim had never met Hugh. He'd seen pictures, and saw him once from a distance when he'd driven by the Matson house on a Saturday afternoon when he knew Hugh was in town. He'd been outside, raking leaves with his son, Craig. Jim had caught only a brief glimpse. He dared to go around the block a second time but realized there was nothing to see. Because no matter how many times he circled, he'd never be able to see Hugh through Donna's eyes.

"Don't get dressed yet," Jim said, getting up and kissing the back of her neck as she leaned over to collect her clothes from the foot of the bed. He smoothed her auburn hair, ran his fingers across her smooth cheek.

"We have to. It's getting late. Carly will be home soon. Stop," she said, turning and pushing him a bit.

How dare she push him like he was some kind of over-eager schoolboy at a dance? "What would you do if I just didn't leave one day?" he said, suddenly angry. "If I just let the whole family come home to find me sitting here on the foot of your bed with a big goddamn hard-on."

"Don't, Jim. You're better than this."

"You're right I am. I'm better than this sneaking around, too, and so are you. We deserve a life together of our own, out in the open."

"And we might have it, Jim. I told you, just not right now. Not while Craig is so young. He's not even in high school yet." She put her cheek against his chest, pulled his reluctant arms up around her. "I don't want to fight."

He didn't either. He wanted to win. And he wanted to win now.

...9

Dear Diary:
A lot to catch you up on! Things seem to suddenly be going my way on all fronts! I had totally given up on Ms. Johns since she completely ignored my note. I was crushed for two weeks, convinced she thought I was a freak and would rat me out to Mom or the school or both. But worse than that, it killed me that she'd stopped talking to me, stopped even calling on me in class! I figured I was must have 180 degrees misjudged her.

But yesterday Fran and I were hanging in the parking lot (more on Fran in a minute!!) and we saw Ms. Johns *getting into her car. Okay, I admit it. I like to watch for her outside of class. I like to see her walking along and getting into her cool car and behaving like a regular person without that desk in front of her. Fran says I have a little crush on Ms. Johns and I deny it because I know it makes her jealous (though I suppose I should want to make her jealous for all the times she's done that — and worse — to me) but she's right, I do. I actually have a BIG crush on Ms. Johns. Can you have a crush on one person while you are in love with someone else? Because I have decided I'm in love with Fran, at least since she has started to be so sweet to me, and we have gone further than we ever had before — but more on that in a minute!*

So Ms. Johns spots us and calls me over and I feel half like I'm going to hurl and half like I could float on air. And I start to tell her to forget everything in my note and she's acting all stern, and then she tells me I could call this group, "Gay Youth," and she hands me this piece of paper (taped below!! it's in her own actual handwriting) with the phone number. And then she makes me swear I won't tell anyone.

Fran and I practically ran all the way to her house and called and both listened in on different extensions. We got this very nice-sounding guy and he told us when the meetings were and said there were a lot of cute girls who came and that everyone just talked about their feelings and problems and made friends.

By the time we hung up, I was giddy. It was like — a whole world of us out there! Not just Fran's three deadbeat friends who dropped out of high school and drink all the time. (Of course, Fran badgered the guy till he gave us the name of a gay bar about 15 minutes from here.) Fran and I talked about how and when we could go to a meeting but we haven't made definite plans yet. She had other things on her mind at that moment, and that was the other thing I wanted to tell you. We were topless together for the first time, and I was in heaven. Her breasts are SO beautiful and silky and the sight of us together like that — I thought I was going to pass out, if a person can pass out from passion!

I have to thank Ms. Johns for the phone number but I don't know where or when it's safe to talk to her about it again. I guess she could get in trouble for doing it. I keep wondering, how did she get the name of the group? How did she know about it? Do you think it's possible, really possible, that she's a lesbian, too? Oh, look what I wrote — "lesbian, too." Do you think this means that I think I am, that I finally accept that I am?

...10

"Carly!" Hugh Matson called up the stairs to his daughter. "What is with the phone ringing every five minutes? Is it a crank caller?" He was trying to relax in the living room, read the paper a bit, catch some of an old movie, and Carly's phone kept ringing like she was running a mail-order business from her room.

He heard her feet pound across the floor. "No, Dad, it's just a friend who keeps calling."

"Well, tell him if you can't make him stop, *I* will. Or just unplug the phone, already!"

"It's a her, not a him. And I don't want my phone out of commission all night."

He sighed and walked back over to the leather recliner. He loved this chair; it was where he pictured himself in the house when he was away in hotel rooms. Normally he pictured Donna on the couch adjacent to him, but she had to go running out tonight, even though he'd gotten back only last night after being gone for the better part of two weeks. You'd think she was the principal, not just a PTO member, the way she was always running and jumping for the school. Sure, he wasn't home a lot, either, but at least he brought home good money to show for it.

He flipped the channels. Animals hunting in the wild. Cooking shows. Music videos. Dumb sitcoms. He switched it off. A loud *poof*, and then the room settled into quiet. Even Carly's phone had stopped ringing. Craig was off playing some kind of video game with the twin boys next door. It did not escape him that his children were not especially interested in him. He blamed himself. He was not especially good with children, and his own had turned out to be no exception. He wished he could just wait till they were adults and then they'd appreciate him, but he knew, from his own father, that it didn't work that way. You had to put in the time, pretending to be interested in the ninetieth game of Monopoly or whatever it was, so that they could bear to go to dinner with you when they were thirty-five.

When Carly was first born, Hugh was impatient for her to talk, so badly did he want to know who she was, what she'd have to say. But then, by the time she was five, he was shushing her constant chatter. The shock had been that she talked like a child, just like other children, about things he didn't, couldn't, care about — games and dolls and other girls' parties. He realized he had once imagined he'd be giving life to a soulmate, to himself only younger and more innocent, less spoiled and ruined, and they would find each other fascinating and figure each other out.

And then she got to be about thirteen, fourteen, and she

was mute again, still as a newborn at meals when Donna would hammer at her, trying to get her to talk. And Carly would dole out these stingy, contemptuous sentences. He found it painful to watch, but he had nowhere to turn. Craig was not a verbal kid, either, and all he seemed to want to do was hurl himself through space and see what he could knock over. Hugh had never been a jock. He had not been the roll-around-in-the-grass-and-bash-your-head-into-the-ground kind of boy when he was young, and he certainly wasn't going to start now, at forty-eight, just to have some way to relate to his son.

Most of the time, Hugh had no idea what his family expected of him. Threatening guys with hard-ons who came to the door looking for Carly was one thing he had imagined he'd be good at, but there hadn't been a boyfriend in sight, something he thought was unusual. Not that he wasn't grateful. After all, he had been a sixteen-year-old boy himself. He'd have humped a grasshopper if he could have figured out how. It amazed him, when he thought about it, how the girls held the guys off as much as they had, and he didn't think girls today even tried to. So every day he was relieved to find that Carly still wasn't pregnant. In his darkest moments he thought this was because she hated him, and he had turned her against all men, and she would become one of those pasty-faced missionaries who never marry.

He felt himself getting morbid, so he turned the TV back on. If Donna had been home, he might have convinced her to go upstairs and screw. He still thought she was great looking, even if the sex was locked into ritual, both of them nearly embarrassed when they came and trying not to make a lot of noise about it. But he still liked sex with her better than he let on.

He knew she was angry with him a lot because he traveled so much, but it wasn't as though he was going off to Tahiti on vacations without her. He was in Sheratons in the Midwest, in meeting rooms with wood laminate conference tables, overeating and overdrinking, making decisions about market share and performance standards that plenty of days meant that some other poor bastard was going to have to fly home and tell his wife they had to sell the house. So what if he screwed some of the sales reps? They all knew he wasn't on the market. It was just an activity, a sport, a diversion, like playing the slots in the lobby casino, or playing b-ball on the night court, only it involved his dick instead of his hands. To him, that didn't constitute being unfaithful. Not that he expected Donna to be grateful about it, and he wouldn't be happy to know she was doing the same. But that was the problem — women never did do it the same way, because they couldn't seem to spread their legs without giving away their hearts.

The younger women were better at leaving their emotions out of it, he'd noticed lately. He tried to stick with the twenty-year-olds, but they weren't as interested in him as they used to be. The thirty-year-olds were the worst, because they were desperate to do the whole marriage thing, wear the big old wedding dress and veil before they were too old not to look ridiculous in it. And the forty-year-olds — well, some of them were okay, especially if they were married, too — but many of them were so busy arranging the sheets so you couldn't see their jiggly thighs or popping stomachs, and he had to spend so much time reassuring them that they made him hard that sometimes he was as limp as steamed broccoli by the time they were finished jabbering.

He heard Donna at the front door and was happy for the distraction; he muted the sound on the TV. "Hi," he called out.

She didn't say anything till she was in the living room, her purse parked, her shoes in the closet. "Where are the kids?" she asked, addressing the television.

"Same place they've been for the last five years, Donna. Somewhere else. Living their own lives. Mostly without us."

She turned slowly, as if looking at him were something she wanted to delay as long as possible. "Speak for yourself," she said.

"It's a new record," he said. "Zero to contempt in less than ten seconds."

"I have to react quickly. You're not in the house long enough for me to take my time."

"Why don't you let me put in a good word for you at work? Then you, too, can enjoy six days and five nights at the fabulous Akron Marriot."

"I'm going to bed, Hugh. As charming as this conversation promises to be, I suddenly don't have the energy for it."

She headed barefoot up the stairs, the carpeted steps creaking as she went. He felt a wild impulse to run after her, smother her in a hug, say he was sorry, beg her to let him take her to bed. But he waited till the urge passed. It was just a fantasy, the idea that his marriage could be what it once was, that they could feel what they once felt, and he couldn't bear trying, right here tonight at the top of the landing, and seeing in her chill look how much they had become strangers. He stayed in his chair, facing the TV, watching shapes and colors moving on the screen, and kept his finger poised over the "mute" button, unwilling to choose what his life would be next, even in the smallest detail.

...11

Fully dressed, Lela had fallen asleep with her laptop on the bed next to her, so when she was awakened by a light rapping sound, she opened her eyes to the weird glow of the swirling screen saver.

At first she thought the sound was rain against the bedroom windows but then, as she came fully awake, she registered the pattern as knocking. Someone was knocking on her door at — she looked at her clock radio — 11:25 p.m. *Who is God's name?* Fear swelled in her throat — was everyone in her family okay? She jogged barefoot to the door, smoothing her jeans and jersey and fluffing her hair as she went.

She peeked through the curtain over the small square window in the door and, in the outside porch light, saw Carly Matson. She was in a purple windbreaker with black tights and turtleneck, hugging her arms to herself and looking over her shoulder at a car idling at the curb.

Lela closed the curtain quickly, panicked. *What in the world...* Just as she considered pretending that she wasn't home, the rapping started again. Lela's breath came in painful stabs. The old terror was wrapping itself around her, the familiar urge to flee pressing in on her. She leaned against the door and swore she could feel the rapping directly at her spine. What if Carly was prepared to stand there the whole interminable night?

Lela threw the door open with more force than necessary, making Carly start. "Oh, Ms. Johns, you *are* home!" the girl said, smiling tremulously. "Am I bothering you? I know it's a little late but I took a chance that you'd be up." Without waiting for a response, Carly turned and waved to the car, which honked, then pulled away. Lela's legs turned leaden at the realization that Carly was inviting herself in.

"Carly, what are you *doing* here?" Lela was squinting in the glare of the porch light, around which dust-speck-sized bugs were flitting.

"I'm bothering you, aren't I?" Carly said, her smile fading. It occurred to Lela from the girl's loose-eyed look and slight sway that she might have had a few beers, unaccustomed ones at that. "Fran and I and some other girls were out at a bar and we were on our way home and I said, 'Hey, can you drop me at Ms. Johns' house? Because I really want a chance to thank her for something wonderful she did.' You know, the phone number. I couldn't thank you at school so —"

"Carly, for God's sake, get in the house," Lela commanded, feeling scaldingly exposed — to Carly, the neighbors, the world. She imagined the curious old woman next door peering out her window to determine who the chatty, late-night visitor was.

Once inside, Carly grew more subdued. No doubt, Lela figured, the girl saw that most of the lights were out and realized how awkward and unwelcome her visit was. Carly hugged her arms tighter to herself. "Um, do you have a bathroom I could use?"

Lela stalked down the hall, with Carly scurrying behind her, and threw on the bathroom light. After Carly shut the door, Lela headed into the kitchen, flicked on the Tiffany-style ceiling lamp and set the kettle to boil. It astounded her that Carly was being so forward. In her own youth, she would never have dreamed of even calling a teacher at home, let alone dropping by unannounced! But everyone these days had gotten so overly familiar, thanks to Oprah and the industry of open-air therapy she'd spawned. Lela saw that she was going to have to be more forceful with the girl, brutal even.

"Ms. Johns?" Carly called out.

"In here," Lela said, not hiding her anger. "I'm making you a cup of coffee and then I'm calling you a cab," she said, pouring the boiled water. "I can't even begin to tell you how completely inappropriate it is that you've come here. How in God's name did you know where I lived, anyway?"

"My mom's on the PTO. She has all the teacher's addresses and phone numbers." Carly was sitting lotus-style on a kitchen chair.

Good *God* — the PTO. What would they have to say about a lesbian teacher having a female student in her house alone at near midnight? "And you just happen to have them all memorized in case you're in the neighborhood?"

Carly gave her a sheepish look. "No, just yours."

"Carly, look, I don't know what ideas you have in your head. But I'm not a social worker, and even if I were, these are nobody's office hours. Now, whatever kind of crisis you've gotten yourself into, you're going to have to get yourself out of it. If giving you that phone number encouraged you to this point, then I bitterly regret it."

Carly's eyes welled with tears. "I'm sorry, Ms. Johns," she whispered. "I'm really, really sorry." She drew a ragged, moist breath. "I'm so embarrassed. I — I think I had too much to drink, and I wasn't really thinking." She laughed nervously. "Oh, my God, you must think I'm an idiot. I've got to leave." She tried to bolt, but Lela grabbed her by the arm.

"Sit down, have your coffee," Lela said. She hadn't been expecting tears. It unnerved her, and moved her, and that unnerved her more. "First things first," Lela said. "Where do your parents think you are and what time are you supposed to be home?"

Carly yanked a napkin out of the holder on the table and noisily blew her nose. "Well, my mom knows who I'm out with, but she thinks we're at the movies. And I'm supposed to be home by midnight."

Lela glanced at her wall clock. Twenty-five minutes left. "How far do you live from here?"

"Um, I'm on Forest, off Rayburn."

That was a ten-minute drive, but if Carly had to wait for a cab, that could easily tack on another fifteen minutes. "Drink some of your coffee and I'll drive you home so you make your curfew," Lela said. "But obviously, don't tell your mother about your little detour."

Carly dabbed at her eyes with trembling fingers. "I'm sorry, Ms. Johns. I won't bother you anymore. I did want to thank you for the phone number, though. That's really all I came by to say. And here you were asleep and everything, and now I feel terrible." Carly picked up her coffee mug; the steam rose up and disappeared into her thick chestnut curls.

"Well, I wasn't asleep, exactly," Lela said, softening. "I was working, and I'm bushed." She ran her hand self-consciously over her hair, hoping she wasn't an eyesore. She had to face the girl in class again, after all, and wanted to retain some semblance of dignity.

"I like your place," Carly said. "It's very cute. Are those couches real velvet?" Carly was craning around the door frame to look into the living room. "My mom would never let us get something that pretty. Everything she buys has to be a fabric that won't get crushed or shiny or stained or whatever. It's like, I think, live a little."

Lela laughed, surprising herself. "I guess it would be unusual to find a teenage girl who gets along with her mother."

"I guess," Carly said, but suddenly all the animation drained from her face. "She'd kill me if she knew I'd been at a bar tonight. Just kill me, and then die herself."

"How did you get in? You're only sixteen, aren't you?"

"This place didn't card." Carly stared down into her coffee mug and pushed her hair behind one ear.

"You're not used to drinking, are you?"

Carly shook her head.

"Look, at the risk of sounding like an old fart," Lela said, "I have to tell you, hardly anything good has ever happened to people who get drunk in bars."

"I know," Carly said thickly. "I was nervous. It was a gay bar. None of us had ever been to one before."

A small jolt of fear made Lela sit up straighter. "How did you happen to find your way to a gay bar?"

"Well, we called that Gay Youth number you gave me."

Shit, Lela thought. "I didn't know that was what the group did — encouraged underage kids to go to bars."

"They didn't. The guy kept telling us to come in for a group talk during the day, and we will, but Fran kind of just kept bugging him for places and he finally caved."

"He shouldn't have," Lela said, her mood darkening. For *her* sake, he shouldn't have. Carly was being too chatty about the place already, and now it was looking like a party hotline. This was the thanks she got for trying to help in some small way.

"We saw some senior girls from Franklin there — that was pretty wild," Carly said. "Except then Fran started flirting with

56

one of them and I got furious. That's when I started yelling at her to take me home. Or to take me here, actually." Her eyes welled up again. "You know, it's hard enough to be in love with another girl, and then she goes and makes it harder. I don't understand why I'm not enough for her."

"Look," Lela said, "let's get you on your way so you don't get into more trouble at home."

Carly took a few last hurried sips of the coffee and they headed out to the carport. Lela turned the car's heat up high; the night air was growing damp. She pulled onto the road.

"Carly, listen to me. Are you listening?"

The girl nodded moodily.

"We're not going to talk about this again, ever. And you're not to be talking about this visit with friends, or the fact that I gave you a phone number. No matter *who* the friends are, you follow? You could get us both into more trouble than you could ever dream."

"I don't understand."

"You don't have to. Just take my word for it."

"You think I'm a freak, don't you?"

"I *don't* think you're a freak. You're *not* a freak — don't let anyone tell you are. Don't ever let anyone control how you feel about yourself. Whether it's Fran or some other kid in school — or even your mother." Her words were so inadequate, she knew, especially in the face of adolescent passions. And yet, self-respect couldn't just be turned over like a baton; it had to be won walking through fire.

They drove a few minutes in silence. Lela turned onto Forest. "Which house is it?"

"One-seventy-seven," Carly said. "Up there, on the right."

It was 12:02, Lela noted with relief as she pulled the car to the curb. The house was set back on a generous lawn and the walk was outlined with tiny garden lights. "Here's another thing you'll just have to take my word for. No one person can ever solve all your problems, and maybe not even any of them. Don't believe anyone who says they can."

"That seems harsh."

"It's the truest thing I know."

"Thank you for not throwing me out, and for talking to me. I wish . . . I wish it didn't have to be the last time."

"You'll be fine, Carly. Good night."

Carly opened the car door but paused before she got out. "I hope you have somebody really nice, who appreciates you."

Lela smiled and waved her out of the car. She waited at the curb till she saw the front door shut safely behind her.

...12

The car that dropped Carly off was not the same one that had taken her away, Donna Matson noted. She had been watching from the dining room window for the last hour. It was too dark to see any detail, but this car was most definitely a different shape, and there were two fewer girls in it than there had been in the car that picked Carly up.

As Donna watched her daughter come up the walk, she felt some tension leave her body. She had changed for bed hours ago — Hugh was away on a business trip — but she knew not to even try to go to sleep till Carly was under her roof for the night. She warmed with relief to see her home now, and yet it was short-lived relief. She waited till Carly closed the door behind her before she came out of the shadows.

"Oh, Mom, you're still up."

Donna knew her daughter was not surprised. "You're late. By a lot. I said eleven fifteen. Do you know what time it is? I've been sick with worry."

"It's hard, Mom, when someone else is driving, to get them to leave exactly when you want them to."

"But that was part of our agreement, wasn't it? You said I didn't have to drive you and pick you up because your friends would get you home on time. I guess I can't let you go out with friends in cars, because you can't judge their character enough to know if they'll take care of you." She was on the stairs, following Carly up to her room.

"They did take care of me, Mom. I'm home in one piece, aren't I?"

"That's not the point. Your responsibility is to get home when I say, no matter what." They were in the bathroom. Donna watched Carly scowling as she put toothpaste onto her brush. "Besides, don't think I didn't notice that you were dropped off by a different car than the one you left in. The car that picked you up was light and bigger. This was a small, dark car."

"It was dark *out*, Mom. It made the car look dark." She was drying her mouth.

"Don't take me for an idiot! I know what a dark car looks like at night, and I know what a light car looks like at night! This was a dark car, and it wasn't the same car you left in. And it wasn't the same number of people. Which leads me to believe you came home with someone totally different. So what the hell went on, Carly?"

"Well, you seem to have it all figured out, Mom, no matter what I say. So why don't you tell me?"

They were both yelling now. "Okay, I'll tell you what. I think you girls picked up boys and you came home with a

60

complete stranger after doing God knows what with him, and you could get yourself pregnant or killed!"

"Oh, God, Mom, *really!*" Carly pushed past her roughly and stomped down the hall to her room.

"Don't you dare push me! And don't you dare slam that door either!"

Carly stormed around the corner into her room, and Donna followed. "If you don't *mind*, Mom, I'd like to get changed and go to bed!"

"Are you having sex, Carly? You don't know the half of it, the things that go on, between AIDS and serial killers and —"

"Mom, *chill!* You don't even know who your own daughter is! *You're* the one fucking around, not me."

Donna stared, and her stomach bucked.

"You think I don't know you're cheating on Daddy?" Carly hissed. "I see you whispering on the phone and making up the bed in the middle of the day. Why don't you save your lectures for yourself?"

Donna sucked in her breath and held it. She felt as though something was squeezing her heart. She took a step, tripped on the foot of the bed and crashed backwards against the wall. Carly looked scared for a second, but she made no move to come forward. "Carly, it's not true . . ." Donna said, hearing her own bewildered whisper.

"Just get out of my room, Mom." Donna was amazed to see her daughter crying. "I don't want to talk about it anymore. We're both tired. I'm sorry I was late."

Donna straightened up. Her throat was raw, as if she'd just shouted across a field. Carly was right. They shouldn't talk anymore tonight. Not because she was tired. But because she was more afraid than she'd ever been in her life.

...13

Dear Diary:

I'm writing this under the covers, with this tiny flashlight-pen. Between that and the fact that I'm still sobbing my eyes out, I can hardly see to write this. I just threw Mom out of my room — I can't believe it! But she just makes me so mad!! Talking to me like I'm some kind of slut! As if I'd be giving it up for those dorky guys at Franklin. She can't even imagine! She'd be grateful if I came home pregnant with triplets if she knew who I was really in love with!

I didn't know for sure about her having an affair. I

didn't even want to admit it here, to you. Because I didn't even want to __think__ about it. But I just accused her of cheating on Daddy and she just about fell over — actually, she __did__ fall over, it was kind of horrible and humiliating — so I guess it must be true. I haven't even had a second to decide how I feel about it. I know they hate each other. You should see what it's like when Daddy's home, which is less and less. They snarl at each other across the dinner table, and think Craig and I don't notice. But I still never really thought she'd cheat on him! I was mostly just looking to distract her from what she was saying to me, and to hurt her somehow if I could. I didn't really expect to sort of plunge right into a vein like that.

A perfect end to a head-pounding night. Fran and I went off to the gay bar that the Gay Youth place told us about. We made out in the back seat all the way there. I was so turned on by the time we got there, I didn't even want to go in. I was ready to go all the way with her, right there in the car in the parking lot. My body was feeling things that — __whoa__ — I didn't even know I could feel! But Fran wanted to go in. She wanted a drink, and she wanted to know who was in there. And sure enough, we're in there less than an hour, and I lose track of her, and when I find her, she's leaning all cozy by the bar with this girl who I know is a senior at Franklin! I just wanted to die. I started crying, and Fran's friend Melissa — who is usually a jerk — actually tried to make me feel better. She told me I was pretty enough to get anyone I wanted and I should just forget Fran. But that just made me more mad, and I stormed over to her and broke them up and made a scene. I'm too embarrassed to even think about it now. I told Fran to drive me to Ms. Johns'.

Well, that really got her attention. "What do you think is going to happen? You think our English teacher is going to take you to bed?" It was so gross, really. Melissa kind of pushed us out of the place into the parking lot, and we were still screaming at each other. I told Fran I just wanted some-

body to talk to me, to treat me right, like they cared — not like she was, one minute telling me she loved me and then literally the next going after another girl.

Ms. Johns was shocked to see me, but then she was really sweet after that. I like her place a lot — she's got **velvet** *couches! She tried to give me advice about Fran, but I don't know if I even remember most of what she said. I was* **pretty toasted** *by then. I lost track of how much I had to drink. I know she swore me to secrecy, said I couldn't ever tell anyone I had been to her place. And I won't tell — I like having her as my own little secret.*

Am exhausted now. Must crash.

...14

Behind the wheel of the car, having just dropped Carly off, Lela was wide awake. She couldn't bear the thought of going home now, lying in bed hearing the dark siren song of the train whistle and the sound of her own crying. She changed course and headed for Kit's.

Kit lived in a small enclave of attached, two-story condos that, with their neat, matching proportions, reminded Lela of honeycombs. When she pulled up in front of Kit's door, she was relieved to spot a light on deep within the house. Maybe Kit had company, but at least she was home. Lela couldn't bear the thought, just then, of being alone.

Kit opened the door and stared.

Lela shrugged. "Would you believe I was just in the neighborhood?"

"Not for a second," Kit said, smiling. "But I'll pretend if that works for you." She stood aside and let Lela enter. "I was just catching up on some work projects. You were the last face I expected to see on my doorstep. At midnight, no less."

"I've just had a late-night visitor myself," Lela said, but when she saw the jolt of jealousy on Kit's face, she quickly explained the circumstances.

"Well, she's nothing if not persistent."

"But what does she want exactly?" Lela asked, exasperated.

"She probably doesn't know herself. Maybe just some friendly association. Maybe she imagines you a worldly older woman who will express-check her out of the chaos of adolescence. Maybe she's got the hots for you and is out of control. Hey, it's the joyful mystery of teaching teenagers, which — it may be cruel to remind you just this second — you chose."

Lela regarded Kit carefully. Her hair was a little matted and she looked drawn. She had probably been working on a design on and off all night, napping and pacing, tearing things up and not being satisfied. It was a syndrome she had described to Lela, and it clearly made her edgy. "You're losing your patience with me, aren't you?"

"Well, the last time I saw you, you left the table a little abruptly, as I recall. I thought maybe I deserved at least an explanation. Unless it was something I said."

Lela smiled weakly. She had put the restaurant fiasco out of her mind. "I'm sorry," she said, sitting down and clasping her hands tightly. "Do you want me to leave?"

"I wish I did," Kit said. "But I just keep wanting you to stay."

"I, uh, didn't want to be alone tonight . . . with this."

"Why does this girl get to you so much?"

"For starters, her mother is on the PTO. If she gets wind of this, they might as well start issuing my unemployment checks right now."

"But it isn't just that." Kit sat down across from her. "Is it? There's something else. You want to help her. Can I say that again without your screaming at me and running from the room?"

Lela started gnawing on the cuticle of her thumb. "*I* don't necessarily want to help her. But I want her to be helped. I can't help her, for one thing. And besides, whoever helped *me*? Whoever helped you, or any of us? No one ever *helps* you with this stuff. You just try to *survive* it."

"No one helped you with *what*, Lela? You've never told me anything about your childhood, or when you came out, or when you first fell in love. Did your parents throw you out of the house? Who broke your heart? Someone did — you aren't hiding that very well, in case you think you are."

"Broke my heart," Lela repeated with sarcasm. "That's what everyone wants — to rush in and put on Band-Aids and be some kind of hero. Well, there *are* no heroes. That's all over. No one gets to fix this." *Stay with me! You promised! You promised! You promised!* She hugged herself to try to stop the trembling, felt more than heard the train whistle like a needle in her ear. She squeezed her eyes shut.

Kit sat next to her and put a bracing arm around her shoulder. "Tell me about it, anyway," she whispered.

Maybe this was what it felt like to want to tell; Lela didn't know anymore. She tried to imagine the words, didn't know how to form them, didn't know where to begin. It wasn't right to ask for sympathy or seek relief or comfort; she hid her face in her hands as she started to cry.

"Tell me anyway," Kit whispered again.

You promised! You promised! You promised!

She needed to run, her breath was coming short and shallow, her neck was damp with sweat. She had to get far away, she had to save herself.

"Tell me."

A girl stood on the hill, scorched grass crunching beneath her sneakered feet. The sun was shining, the sky stretched blue in all directions. Behind her was a girl on the railroad tracks.

"Her name was Natalie," Lela began.

Part II

10 years earlier

...15

"Natalie, come up to the front of the room, please," Sister Kathleen said in her cool, disapproving tone.

Lela felt her stomach contract like an accordion. She watched, without turning her head, as Natalie hesitated for one defiant moment, then rose and walked slowly down the row between the black-topped science lab tables. She stood next to Sister Kathleen, her hands behind her back, regarding the class as someone might before an address, rather than before a major reaming out.

"Can you tell the class why you feel you have the right to

disrupt everyone's education with whispering and joking and general disrespect?"

Lela pressed her fist against her mouth, wishing she could tear her eyes away. Natalie was looking over everyone's heads, full at her, a smile playing around the corners of her lips. Lela felt her face go hot, knowing what was in Natalie's mind: the thought of the two of them yesterday, in Natalie's bed, clothes more off than on, light-headed with their own daring and desire. And now Natalie was standing up there in front of everyone, smiling at her while Sister Kathleen glared from one to the other of them.

"What is it, Natalie? Are you trying to implicate Miss Johns in your shenanigans?" Half the class craned their necks to gape at Lela. She quickly looked down, but she heard the synchronized swish of their starched uniforms as they turned in unison. She was stiff with fear, but there was also something else: a new thrill, a pride, that everyone would now know of her association with Natalie Sheehan. "That's classic, Natalie, for a troublemaker — to try to drag others down with her, which is what you do when you disrupt the class with your sophomoric behavior and stop us all from doing what we're here to do, which is to teach and to learn."

"I'm sorry, Sister," Natalie said. "I'm just in a good mood today. High spirits, my mother calls it." She turned to confront the nun, the high beam of her charm fully on. Lela didn't see how it was possible for anyone not to be disarmed.

Lela raised her eyes again to take in her lover — and she loved using that word, hearing Natalie breath it against her earlobe. Natalie's hair was caramel-colored, long around her shoulders. She was fine boned, from her cheeks to her wrists, and yet she was sturdy and tall, like a new tree sure of its future strength. Lela at first hadn't thought of Natalie as pretty, but that was before she loved her. Now she marveled at her nearly too-light blue eyes and gold lashes, the faint spray of freckles that Lela swore she now knew the arrangement of by heart, the small mouth that added a note of cunning.

"A sunny disposition is a gift from God, Natalie, but what you are doing in class today is an abuse of that. It's borishness and selfishness, the marks of an undisciplined mind. I will pray tonight that you benefit from the influence of Miss Johns, and not the other way around. Now, since you are determined not to be interested in our lesson, you are excused, Natalie. But you are expected to make up the work on your own, or else suffer the consequences on the midterm next week."

"But, Sister, I —"

"Always sorry too late, Natalie. That won't work with me. Go gather up your belongings and leave."

The girls, seated three to a lab table, seemed to wilt. A certain sense of possibilities would leave the room with Natalie, and they all, with the exception of the few of the most remotely brilliant girls, would miss her. Natalie came back to her seat next to Lela and scooped up her books; Lela could smell the warm, woody saltiness of her skin. As Natalie reached for her pen, she let her pinkie graze the side of Lela's hand. "I'll wait for you," Natalie mouthed, but Sister Kathleen saw it and pounced.

"*Now*, Natalie."

As Natalie walked across the front of the room and out the door, Sister Kathleen kept her gaze fixed on Lela. It was hard to guess at what the nuns were ever thinking, but Lela thought she read clearly the look on Sister Kathleen's face: profound surprise.

"I'm burning up," Natalie was saying into Lela's ear; her words registered as physical sensation more than sound. Lela was half on top of her, both their plaid school skirts flung upward. Lela's legs were trembling and her neck was clammy.

She was touching Natalie the way Natalie had shown her, the way Natalie touched her. Beneath her underpants, Natalie felt like fruit, a summer peach, sticky and slippery soft. Lela wanted to look but she was afraid. "I'm burning up, make me catch fire," Natalie was whispering.

Lela's heart was thumping with urgency. She repositioned her finger, hoping to discover the groove that Natalie had found so easily on her.

"Here, lover," Natalie said in a strange new husky voice. She put her own hand over Lela's, mixed her fingers with Lela's and pushed them toward some stem, directing her in a glide, up and down, faster and faster. Then she made a sound like she had been punched, and she squeezed her thighs tightly together. Her body relaxed in one long shudder.

Natalie rolled over, so that she was now looking down at Lela, her gold hair tickling Lela's nose. "I am *so, so, so, so* in love with you," Natalie said. "I didn't care if everyone in class today knew it, Sister Kathleen included."

This kind of talk terrified Lela, even as it thrilled her. "We can't let them know, Natalie. They'll keep us apart."

"Don't you know no one can keep us apart? No one. Nothing. Not even death."

Lela reached up, tucked Natalie's hair behind her ear. "I never want to be without you."

"You mean that completely?"

"As much as I know how." And it was true: she had done all kinds of things for Natalie she never, ever thought she would do for anyone. Let Natalie copy her biology homework, broke up with Brian, defied her mother by lying about her whereabouts. In fact, she'd invented a whole fantasy after-school life that involved her and Natalie and scores of others working on the yearbook together, when the truth was she went again and again to Natalie's house, to Natalie's bedroom, while Natalie's parents were both at work.

"You're the only one who's ever made me feel worth anything," Natalie said, her eyes — to Lela's amazement — suddenly shiny with tears.

"Stop it! I'm the one lucky to be with you! You're the star of the basketball team, the most popular girl in the junior year, maybe even the whole school. *Everyone* loves you."

"No, they don't. Sure, they're happy enough to go along for the ride for a while. But no one's stood by me for the long haul. Sooner or later I'm too much trouble. But you stared down ol' Sister Katie today. I was *amazed*."

Lela lifted her head and kissed Natalie. "Anyone who doesn't love you can't know you."

Natalie pulled away and sat up. "It's not true. You love me because you don't know everything about me."

"What are you saying?" Lela asked, her heart tapping high in her throat.

Natalie scowled across the room. "I was in a nuthouse once. Last summer. My parents checked me in."

"What do you mean? I don't understand." Lela scrambled over and nestled as close to Natalie as she could. "Tell me," she said, afraid when Natalie's eyes welled with tears.

"I, I have these moods. Or I did. It's what my mother calls the high spirits. I pulled a picture off the wall once and threw it at her. There was glass all over. She dragged me off to this place and they stuck me with needles and made me take drugs for two weeks. And now I have to take these pills all the time. But I don't always take them, not that I tell my mom that. Because I don't ever really feel happy when I'm on the pills." Natalie took Lela's face in both her hands. "And I want to feel every last drop of happiness now that I have you."

"Wait a minute — you're supposed to take pills and you're not taking them? Do you need them? What are they for? You're scaring me. I don't want anything to happen to you! What if they drag you off again and I can't get in to see you and they don't send you my letters and —"

"Shhhh!" Natalie said, laughing. "None of that's going to happen. No one's going to know but you and me. I need the pills only when I'm sad or angry, but now that I'm with you, that'll never, ever happen. Don't you see? You've cured me."

75

Goose bumps ran down Lela's arms. She'd never known anyone . . . anyone what? Crazy? Was Natalie crazy? No, anyone who thought so was crazy. Anyone could see what a strong and sweet and passionate person Natalie was. If Natalie was crazy, everyone would be lucky to be as crazy. "What made you so mad at your mom?"

Natalie hugged her knees up against her chest. "I don't know — nothing and everything. She hates that I play basketball. Says it's not ladylike. And she wants me to be smarter. Like my brother, who's going to be a doctor. He's a resident up in Boston. He's ten years older than me. He's all my parents ever talk about. I don't even know him. He could be operating on me one day and I might not even recognize him." At this, Natalie broke into hyena laughs and fell across Lela's lap. Then she stopped just as abruptly. "But I don't want to talk about any of this," she said, getting up and going to the window. "I don't want you to know any more about it. You won't love me if you know it all."

"That's crazy," Lela said, instantly regretting her choice of words.

Natalie whirled around. "See, it's starting already. You'll wonder about everything I do and say now and think it's an *imbalance* — that's what they all call it, like I'm some kind of scale."

"I won't, I'm not, that's not what I meant. I love you just the way you are, and every way you ever will be." Lela jumped up and crushed herself against Natalie from behind. And she meant it with every last ounce of strength she had. Even if Natalie did have some kind of problem — that was what love was about, cherishing the whole person and helping them through.

"Don't say it if you don't mean it, Lela," Natalie said, turning to face her.

"But I do. Completely. I'd, I don't know, I'd *die* if I couldn't be with you," Lela said, her voice quavering with conviction.

And then Natalie kissed her, long and slow. Lela tasted tears, but she couldn't be sure whose they were.

"Lela, please, wait for a moment," Sister Kathleen said as the class was filing out.

They had spent the hour reviewing the material for Friday's midterm, and everyone was a little subdued. Lela most of all, because Natalie had stayed home. Lela had called her from the hall pay phones four times already. Natalie said she felt nauseous, but Lela worried it had something to do with the pills. Every time she tried to ask, though, Natalie got angry and wouldn't answer. Instead, Natalie pleaded with Lela to cut classes, to take the bus to the big empty house where she was in her bed, waiting to kiss her all over, along the insides of her thighs the way Lela had just discovered she loved.

"Lela, sit down," Sister Kathleen said. Lela settled into a front-row seat and felt her breath come in short, stabbing pains. She'd never been in any trouble before, ever; the nuns had only ever praised her and held her up as an example. "I'm glad to have this chance to talk to you alone, Lela, without Natalie Sheehan attached to your hip."

Lela felt her face go hot as a skillet.

"Because I meant what I said in class the other day," the nun went on, "about hoping that you would have an effect on Natalie, and not the other way around."

Lela stared at her feet. "Natalie is a good person," she said, freighting the sentence with as much indignation as she dared.

"God makes only good people, Lela, but they nonetheless find ways to go astray. Now, if you are finding that Natalie blooms under your influence, then maybe you are more saintly than a lot of us have been. But I do worry, given what a forceful and charismatic personality she is, that there is the danger that she'll implicate you in her troubles. You are, after all, only human, Lela, but you're too fine a student for us just to stand by and wait for the worst to happen."

Lela looked up slowly, trying to absorb all of what the nun was saying, and at least some of what she wasn't. Mainly she was trying to adjust to the fact that the nun had thought this much about them. Forceful and charismatic — *wow!* Wait till she told Natalie! But what did Sister Kathleen suspect, exactly? What did she mean by "the worst"? Could she have seen the way they'd been looking at each other, and figured it all out? No, it wasn't possible, Lela decided, examining the nun's pasty face and droopy eyes and slightly furred upper lip. Sister Kathleen would have been shocked beyond comprehension if she'd even imagined how Lela was craving Natalie even now, craving the dark dampness between her thighs . . .

"I understand, Sister," Lela said, forcing herself to sit up straighter, hoping it signaled an eagerness to go home and study biology.

"Hmmm," Sister Kathleen said, folding her arms. "I wonder if you do."

Lela stood up and looked the nun in the eye. They were the same height; she'd never noticed that before. She wondered now: Did the whole faculty know about Natalie's pills? Was that what the hints were about? "Am I dismissed?" Lela asked finally.

The nun waved her out of the room without smiling. Lela knew, however, that she was watching her go.

"That witch!" Natalie shouted. Lela was alarmed; she'd thought Natalie would be as flattered by the nun's description as Lela had been for her. "Don't you see what she's trying to do? Turn you against me!"

"Well, of course she is," Lela said, scuttling behind Natalie, trying to keep up with her frantic pacing. "You pissed her off and she's a nun. What do you expect?"

Natalie stopped in her tracks. "What do I *expect*? For everyone to leave us alone! Who the hell do they all think they are? This is the first time I've ever really been happy in my life and they're all out to ruin it!" Natalie suddenly hunched over and began sobbing into her hands. Lela wrapped her arms around her, trying to extinguish her grief, like a blanket on a flame.

"Stop, it's okay, I'm here," Lela said, crying a little, too, and for too many reasons than she could sort out. If they were adults, away at college, she and Natalie could work this all out by themselves. It was the constant threat of discovery that was getting to them. Natalie would be *fine* if they would all just leave them alone.

Natalie grabbed Lela's face and kissed her hard, mashing their lips and banging their teeth. She toppled them onto the bed and began to unbutton Lela's blouse and pull it free from her skirt. The spiral of desire began to spin up from Lela's groin.

"Natalie! Natalie, I'm home early. How are you, honey?" came a voice from downstairs.

"Oh, shit! Goddamn it all to hell!" Natalie said, scrambling to her feet. "It's my mom! Get dressed." She was trying, in comic-book warp speed, to wipe her face dry and straighten Lela's clothes all at once. Lela had never met Mrs. Sheehan, and her heart sank at the thought of meeting her now, like this.

"I came home early to see how you were feeling," the voice said, ascending the stairs.

When Natalie saw that Lela was settled and sitting on the bed, she rushed to the door and threw it open. "Hi, Mom. I have a friend over. She's helping me with the biology class notes I missed, since we're having the midterm Friday."

Mrs. Sheehan, shorter and blunter than her daughter with ruddy cheeks and a sensible short haircut, came into the room and frankly sized up Lela with the same pale blue Sheehan eyes. Lela stood and managed a hello.

"This is Lela, Mom. She took the bus over from school,"

Natalie said, turning to beam at Lela. Even across the room, Lela could feel Natalie's pride in her, in their love.

"Oh, well, isn't that nice of you?" Mrs. Sheehan said, and Lela had no real way of knowing if she meant it. "Didn't quite get to break the books out yet, though?" she said, scanning the closed backpack, the rumpled bed and her daughter's blotchy face.

"No, she just got here, Mom."

"Yakking about boys or some such first, I guess, huh?" Mrs. Sheehan said, smiling at Lela.

They all laughed then, as if on cue, but Lela didn't feel the tension leave the room.

"I suppose you must feel better if you're up to company then, Natalie?"

"It's not company, Mom. We're studying. But yeah, I do feel better."

"Well." The short woman looked around the room once more. "Don't see any reason to keep yourselves shut in, then," she said, pushing the door open wider. "I'll bring up some tea," she said, reaching up and feeling Natalie's forehead in a gesture that struck Lela as more medical than maternal. "If you need a lift home later, Lela, I'll be happy to drive you so you don't have to mess with the bus again. And thank you for helping my daughter with the midterm." She turned and looked back at Natalie as she headed for the stairs. "We all want her to do as well as she can."

Lela tore off the wrapping and stared at the black velvet box. She and Natalie were around the corner from school, safely away from the bus stop, where everyone was sure to be talking about their plans for spring break. It was the first day that hinted at the coming warm weather, and everyone had underdressed in anticipation. Lela, sitting on the curb under a newly blossoming pear tree, shivered a little in her windbreaker.

"What is this?" Lela asked. She knew from the box's heft and plushness that this was no drugstore trinket.

"It's our six-month anniversary — or did you forget?" Natalie said.

This was how everything was becoming now, laced with accusation, a dare to betrayal. Lela was doing and saying everything she could think of to reassure Natalie, but she was beginning to worry that nothing would ever be enough. "Of course I haven't forgotten. I just mean —"

"Just open it, beautiful," Natalie said, springing on her toes as she paced.

Lela cracked the box open cautiously and saw the gleam first, as the sun reflected off the gold. When she angled it, she could make out the necklace's thick and intricate link, its heavy, lobster-claw clasp. This was the real thing, an adult piece of jewelry of the kind she saw advertised in glossy magazines and had no idea who could afford. She stared speechless and could think of nothing to say.

"Do you love it?" Natalie demanded.

"I do, but how —"

"I want you to wear it twenty-fours hours a day. I never want you to take it off. So you'll think of us always."

"But Natalie —" Lela couldn't imagine ever wearing the necklace, at least not in public, not without being in a self-conscious sweat. Maybe she could wear it one day, twenty years from now, if she ever got to meet the President of the United States. The only jewelry she owned was a stainless steel spoon ring and a cheap chain on which she alternated a starfish pendant and a cross. She could no more wear this necklace than she could do a striptease on the science lab tabletop. "How did you *afford* this?"

"Come here," Natalie said, dragging her over to sit on the brick steps that led down a garden to the rectory. "My mother gets all kind of junk mail. I open some of it and I just applied for a credit card in her name and *voilà* — it came! So I went shopping for you at Jordan's and charged it. And the best part is we're going to use the card to go away for a while, too. I don't know how long, maybe forever. I thought maybe we could go live in Amsterdam or someplace where women love other women all the time and no one thinks anything of it. I've been reading about it. I wanted to wait till our anniversary to surprise you. I want to kiss you right here, right now, Lela Johns."

Natalie had her arms folded across her knees and was resting her head on her arms, grinning, innocent as a puppy. Even Natalie's optimism wasn't enough now to keep Lela from feeling the weight of sadness bear down on her. She felt certain all at once that Natalie would be leaving soon, whether Lela went with her or not. She would have to be without her, then, after all, and no one would have done it to them. Natalie would end up doing it herself. She struggled to stop herself from crying but couldn't.

"Honey, what's the matter?" Natalie asked, the pitch of her voice spiking with alarm.

"How are we going to pay for this?" She had the necklace box open before her, like a clam.

"Don't worry about that. They send bills, and I keep picking them up from the mailbox so my mom will never know. All I've got to do is pay them a little bit at a time and I can practically take forever. I make enough baby-sitting to pay them what they want each month. Or," she said, lifting the necklace out of its black satin bed, "we could be halfway across the world by then and they'll never find us with their stupid bills."

"Natalie, stop," Lela said, grabbing Natalie's wrist. "I don't care about expensive things. I only want you." She looked pleadingly into Natalie's eyes, praying she'd understand and not take it as another sign of her lack of commitment. "I don't want us getting into trouble with bill collectors or being chased by truant officers or FBI agents or whatever. We're going to do this by the rules, start our life together right. Nobody will have anything to hold against us but our love, and by then, we'll be too old for them to stop us."

"Oh, Lela, you always expect the best of people. It's what

I love about you. But it's also why I have to protect you. Don't you see? Between your mother and my mother and Sister Kathleen and who knows who else, no one's going to let us live our life. And if somebody does find out, well, there's a perfect reason to throw me back in the cuckoo bin —"

"You're exaggerating. No one is going to find out if we're careful, and wearing this necklace is not what I'd call careful! I mean, I might as well wear a neon *L*. Sometimes I think you're *trying* to get us caught."

"You're doing it."

"Doing *what*?" Lela asked.

"Trying to psychoanalyze me the way the doctors do because no one thinks I can be expected to know myself what I'm thinking."

"That's ridiculous. Even normal people have motives they hide from themselves."

"Even *normal* people!" Natalie shot up and staggered back a few steps.

"Oh my God, Natalie. Natalie, I didn't mean it like that." Lela tasted acid at the back of her throat. "Natalie, Natalie, it just slipped out, it's an expression — I didn't mean anything by it." She took a few steps forward, trying to reach out for Natalie's hand, but Natalie kept backing away and jerking her head like a horse before it bolts.

"Even you, Lela . . ." Natalie said.

"No, no, noooooo!" Lela screamed, but Natalie had taken off down the block, sprinting like a woman running for her life.

For the entire week of midterm break, Natalie did not return a single one of Lela's calls. Lela considered going over to her house, but she was afraid, by turns, of the humiliation if Natalie were home but didn't answer the door, and the disappointment and fear if Natalie really wasn't there. She fantasized the worst: that the entire family had moved, that Mrs. Sheehan had checked Natalie back into the hospital, that Natalie had taken up with some other girl. She swung sickly back and forth between remorse, guilt, terror, rage, lust, pride. She was cold to her parents, ignored her cat, Mr. Biscuits, and cruel to her little brother. She stroked the necklace, tried it on with every blouse and dress she owned. She cried herself to sleep at night. She learned how to touch herself and fantasized about Natalie's body. She went over and over in her head what she would say to Natalie when she finally talked to her again: *I'll do anything, anything it takes to prove I love you. I'll run away with you. I'll quit school* (though she always, in her mind, planned to come back). *I'll rob banks to feed us.* There would be hell to pay and her life would possibly be in tatters for a while, but nothing was worse than this — being without Natalie.

The Sunday before school started again Natalie finally called. Lela locked the door to her room and got into bed with the phone. "Don't ever do that to me again, Natalie Sheehan," Lela announced with hard-won righteousness.

"I couldn't help it," Natalie said, her voice flat. "It hurts too much to talk to you if I know you're thinking I'm crazy, because then it's just a matter of time before you leave me, too."

"I'm wearing the necklace. I've been wearing it every day. Most of the time it slips under my blouse so my mom hasn't noticed it. And I'm not leaving you. *Ever.* Who are all these people who've abandoned you? It's not right that you keep grouping me in with them."

"Who? They're all around, that's who. Starting with my parents. Locking me up in the loony bin. They didn't even want to take me home after the two weeks, even though the doctors said they could."

"Your mother's a nurse — she believes in medication and hospitals, that's why."

"Believes in them for what — raising your kids?"

"What did they say was wrong with you anyway? What are the pills for exactly?"

"They threw all kinds of terms around. Bipolar disorder. Manic depression. Plain old depression. The pills are called lithium. All I know is that they're like a straight jacket on my brain. I can't really feel happy on them. I don't feel my black moods either, but Lela, no one should have to live without happiness, should they?"

Lela felt such a swell of joy and possessive love, such a ferocious attachment, that she couldn't force mere words through it. "No, they shouldn't, angel, and you won't ever have to. You'll always have me, for as long as you want."

"And there was a girl, there, too, in that place. I didn't love her like I love you, but she was my first. She was older, and she had dropped out of college. We would sneak off and find places to be alone. One time we went to the roof at night after we found a broken door that didn't trip the alarm. We used our shirts as blankets to lie down on. I don't know what they would have done if they'd found us. Probably given us lobotomies or something. She had a boyfriend on the outside, where she lived, way out on Long Island, and when we both got out we wrote a few times but then in one letter she told me she was getting engaged. She said what we did and felt together was sick and evil, worse than any of the things they were treating us for, and she was never going to think about me again."

Hot tears streamed down the side of Lela's nose. She was hot all over, in a jealous fever that Natalie had loved someone before her. But she was also afraid. Could the things this other girl said be true? Would she never have a love like this for her whole life? Would she have to go be with someone like Brian when the most she felt for him was abstract respect for his terrific grades and pleasant singing voice at church? "Well, she was a coward and an idiot, and I hope she's miserable," Lela said, a fury building inside her. "I'm not marrying anyone but you, and I'll do whatever it takes to prove it to you."

"I don't know if I can do it, baby."

"What do you mean?" Lela said, struggling upright in bed.

"Go to school, play the trained seal for people like Sister Kathleen. I just don't give a shit about any of it. I haven't even gone to a single b-ball practice. Sister Jean has left me a thousand messages, too. I think I quit the team. Sort of by default. I haven't called her back."

"Put the phone closer to your mouth, Natalie. I can't hear you all the way. You need to take those pills, please, even just a half, just something. You've got yourself in a funk, that's all."

"Too late. I dumped the latest supply down the toilet."

Lela's heart was clattering around in her chest. Maybe she should tell her mother? Maybe she should tell Mrs. Sheehan? Or Sister Kathleen, or someone. No, it would be no use. None of them had been able to help before. And Natalie really would never speak to her again for betraying her to them. She couldn't risk it. She was so in love her insides hurt. She was the only one who could save Natalie — and she would. "I'm coming over right now," Lela said, on her feet.

"No, don't. They're all here. My brother's visiting, down from the heavens. You can hardly see across the room, that's how bright the halo is on his head. And he has some girl with him. I think they're going to get married. He will deliver unto her his superhuman sperm and they will beget superhuman genius babies who will grow up and save all the world from blight and suffering."

"Natalie . . ." Lela would have laughed, had everything been normal, had she been sure Natalie was all right. But she was sure of nothing now.

"All I want to do is get under the covers with you and . . . I can't even tell you the things I've imagined.

Constantly," Natalie said. "You're a record on in my head all the time now. Except I can't really have you."

Lela felt lightheaded; this is what she needed to hear Natalie say. "You *can* have me. Totally, even more than we've been so far. Let's go away, like you said. Tell me the plan. We won't even go back to school tomorrow. We'll be on a plane."

Natalie was silent. Lela imagined she was thinking it over. "I don't think anymore . . . that even Amsterdam is far enough."

"What could be farther?" Lela was scanning the room, wondering how many of her things she could pack in a bag small enough to sneak away with and not attract much attention from her mother. Her mother would take care of Mr. Biscuits. She'd get to Amsterdam, or wherever, she'd get Natalie back to normal, and then she'd come back home with her and explain to everyone why they had to do it, and she'd be forgiven, and everything would go on as usual.

"Farther is . . . oblivion."

"What are you talking about?" Lela focused all her attention on Natalie's voice again.

"I've been thinking about . . . about obliteration. About us together on the railroad tracks. It would be easy, fast. Because that's the only way I can see that we can be together, and happy."

"You're not *serious,*" Lela said. She was emptied out, sucked dry and filled back up, packed full with fear.

"I am. Dead serious, in fact." Natalie began laughing and didn't stop. Lela squeezed her eyes shut and tried to imagine that they were laughing together, about something else.

"We *can* be together, *damn* you, Natalie. Where's your fight?"

"I've *been* fighting, lover. Longer than you've known me. I'm tired now. Tired, tired, tired. If you come with me, we'll die happy, and we'll be happy together forever. That's all you can do for me, now."

"I'm not going to let you die, Natalie."

"I've got to go. They're calling me for dinner. I'll see you at school tomorrow. I'll meet you after history class."

"Okay." History was Lela's last class. They had a copy of each other's schedule. Natalie couldn't really be planning a regular day of classes if she was going to kill herself at the end of it, could she? It had been a hard week for them both, being apart; it had just made Natalie morbid. But tomorrow they would go back to Natalie's room and they would be totally alive together and this would all be forgotten, this dark talk. After all, Lela had never known anyone who actually tried to kill herself, never even knew someone who knew someone. She even gave in to a smile as she hung up. It had been very scary but now it was over.

She ran her finger slowly back and forth over the smooth, cool links of her gold necklace, making plans. They wouldn't have to run away, she wouldn't have to leave her family or drop out of school. She would make love to Natalie in a way that made her never think of that girl in the hospital again, in a way that kept her happy all the time. And it would all begin tomorrow.

Lela checked her watch every five minutes for the last half of history class, nervous and excited about seeing Natalie. Her *lover*. They hadn't been apart this long in months. She had run from homeroom to meet her before her first class, just to be sure she was in. Natalie looked thin, a little pale, and without her usual mischievious spark. Lela pulled back the collar of her blouse to show Natalie that she was wearing the necklace. Natalie beamed, and Lela half seriously considered kissing her right there in the hallway, so relieved was she at the sight of her, the fact of her, and the simple phenomenon of Natalie's smile, intended for her.

When the bell rang for the class's end, Lela had her books already stacked, and she flew from her seat. She spotted Natalie easily, taller than most of the girls, coming down the hallway. She ran to meet her. "Come on," she whispered. "I can't wait to get you alone."

But Natalie didn't break her pace and said nothing till they were out in the courtyard, the sun in their eyes. "We're not going home. I told you where we're going today."

Lela stopped short and the crowd parted around them. She felt the ground tilt, and the moment slow down till it froze. "Where are we going?"

"To the railroad tracks. I told you." Natalie kept walking. "I knew you didn't believe me."

Lela jogged to catch up, feeling queasy with each step that put her farther from the school and possible help. How could it be that the nightmare was back? "I won't let you, Natalie."

"The only thing you can do is not let me do it alone, baby. And I've prayed you'll come with me. Because then we'll have forever. But if you don't, you'll stay with all the rest of them, without me." She waved her hand as if to include St. Ignatius, Oakwood, the whole world.

It was more than a mile to the tracks, and Lela held her breath for as long as she could. When she couldn't bear it any longer, when she felt the press of tears would send her eyes straight out of their sockets if she held them back anymore, she let herself start to cry. They had come to an unfenced meadow and, limp with fear, she threw herself down on the grass and cried for everything she was about to lose. How could she live if Natalie died without her, if she turned down Natalie's last request? How could she send Natalie into eternity and fail the ultimate test of true love? How could she live *without* Natalie? How could the world go on without her? It *couldn't*. But how could she die, either, on an ordinary, sunny day, without warning, without even a chance to say good-bye to anyone? She thought of the distracted kiss she'd given her mother this morning . . . and she'd been mean to Mr. Biscuits all week. She was coughing up tears now, and a little bit of her breakfast, and her guts.

"Lela," Natalie said, sitting down beside her and stroking her back. "I know it's scary, but you won't regret it. Not if you really love me."

Lela tried to concentrate only on the sweet timbre of Natalie's voice and the feel of her touch on her back, out here in the open, under the sun. "Let's go to your room and —" Lela said, having to suck in her breath to get her voice under control — "and make love. I don't want us to die." She buried her face in her hands and rocked.

"Come on," Natalie said, tugging at her wrist. "I have the train schedule memorized. We don't have time to spare. I don't want to miss this one and have to wait for the next."

Lela stumbled to her feet and continued pleading, not recognizing the hysterical scratchy sound of her own voice, unable to think of what to say to dent such resolve. The swill in her stomach kept rising and she had to stop several more times, to Natalie's growing impatience, to spit up bile. *"You can't do this!"* Lela shouted, hoping someone in one of the neat ranch houses along their route would hear her and come out to see what all the commotion was about. But no one stirred and no one came. "If *you* really loved *me*, you wouldn't do this," Lela accused.

"It's the only safe, true way for us to be together, Lela." Natalie was holding her hand in a tight, sweaty fist, dragging her along. She didn't seem to care who saw them. "I can't fight them all anymore. This is the only way we can win."

And then it was in front of them, the sloping hill down to the railroad tracks. The tracks looked innocent, too neutral and functional to have any power to harm, and at the same time so sinister and lethal that Lela felt awed and defeated. How was it that the tracks were out here, so exposed, so accessible to anyone with a death wish?

Natalie looked at her watch. "It should be coming around this bend now in . . . mmmm, about three and a half minutes."

Lela sagged to her knees and the sky spun over her head. She wrapped her arms around Natalie's legs, but her crying had fatigued her and she was no match for Natalie's strength as she half dragged, half carried Lela down to the tracks.

"Angel, I'm not going to force you," Natalie said when they were close enough to touch the tracks, to smell the mossy earth under them. "I'm not going to tie you down or hold you. I'm only going to remind you of your promises to me."

Natalie's eyes were startlingly blue and gorgeous, Lela realized all over again. They were commanding her. She allowed herself to be led on to the tracks, and she was grateful, happy, relieved to lie down next to Natalie, to smell the sun on her skin, to kiss her soft, moist lips, her delicate eyelids, the tiny gold hairs at her hairline. "Forever," they whispered in turn, and they clung to each other as the tremor began underneath them, reaching to claim them from a long way off.

"Natalie, I love you," Lela said, her words shattered into mere atoms by the first blast of the train whistle. She looked across Natalie's chest and saw the train's blunt, black head and its single bright eye, and then she was being lifted, her body nearly weightless. The train whistle shot into her skull like an arrow and the air around her shook and rumbled as if it were a physical thing, tumbling apart. Her body was vibrating with sound, her teeth were clattering, and she wondered how it was that she could hear anything at all over the racket. But she could, and it was Natalie's screams: *"Where are you going? Stay with me! You promised!"* till her voice turned into the whistle itself and Lela ran and ran and ran and ran.

Part III

...16

Donna Matson had never done anything like this before, but then again, that seemed to be becoming the theme of her life. Never had she cheated on Hugh, either, or thought of leaving him, or felt so exasperated by Carly that she thought she might strike her. But life was full of firsts these days, it seemed. Not good, happy firsts like when she'd gotten married or had her babies, or when they 'd bought the house. No, now the firsts were all failings, and her little mental score card mocked her. She had become a person she didn't fully recognize, a person whose values she would have once — and, still would — object to passionately in public, a person she would not have wanted to associate with.

And today she was adding another first: she had woken up that morning knowing she was going to raid Carly's room. Some parents might not have thought much of it, might even consider it their due or responsibility, but Donna didn't. To do it meant that you no longer trusted your child and, given that you would have to act on whatever you found (or else what would be the point?) your child would no longer trust you. It meant that you were no longer capable of communicating with your child, that you were closer to being hostile strangers than mother and daughter.

How else to explain the way Carly talked to her and looked at her, Donna wondered, stirring her second cup of coffee for the morning. How had she guessed at the affair? Had she and Jim been that sloppy? She hadn't thought so. Making up the bed in the middle of the day — she always used to do that. Laundry was an afternoon chore. And whispering on the phone? She didn't think she had done that. Was her own guilty conscience sending out such clear brain waves that her own daughter had been able to make a good guess? And if so, why hadn't Hugh? Or had he noticed, too, and just didn't give a damn.

She leaned forward at the beige kitchen nook table, put her head in her hands and willed herself not to cry. One warm tear escaped and streaked down her cheek. Maybe she should get a job sooner than she planned. But Craig was only seven; she had hoped to wait three more years. Even so, maybe this was a sign from God. She was too idle. That was what lead her to discontent with her husband, and time to fall in love with another man.

At the thought of Jim, she felt herself stir with desire. She was appalled at herself, really. She seemed to want him — physically — more and more. She had hoped that might wane, and then separating from him might be possible. But their lovemaking — she had stopped, somewhere along the way, thinking of it as just sex — had ripened into something truly virtuoso, and she had marveled at the depth of her appetite. Her first thought at Carly's accusation was to call Jim immediately and tell him it had to end, but then she was ashamed, deeply ashamed, to find herself paralyzed before the phone, unable to make the sacrifice, even for the sake of her daughter's moral life. The next time he called, she told him about the ugly fight with Carly, but the idea of ending their affair was as distant as some half-remembered dream whose logic, in the clear light of day, escaped her.

She got up from the table to look out her kitchen window and take stock of the state of the bird feeders. Yes, they would need refilling today, and the flower beds were overdue for weeding. Of course, Jim had repeated again his desire to marry her, and she had fallen so completely into the habit of saying no, saying that it couldn't be, that she didn't even think about the words anymore. It had become a dance they were practiced in, requiring no real attention. But she allowed herself the truly heretic thought now: *what if?* She imagined herself out in public with Jim — at the supermarket, at a PTO meeting (he, of course, would come, whereas Hugh never had), at the local movie theater. And might their friends remark, "Donna, you look so happy. We wondered how long you could take it — with Hugh away so much, and God knows he never appreciated you anyway." And what would it be like to go out to dinner, and eye each other openly across their wineglasses, and know that when she got home, he would undress her slowly and kiss her shoulders and open her up in a way she had never felt with a man before? What would it be like to be happy?

But it wasn't that simple, not at all. She wanted all this with Jim, but she wanted it in another life, one that she could start afresh, or in a parallel universe she could visit at will. Because she did not want to be divorced. She did not want to be the one to say to Hugh that she had been unfaithful. She did not want to be to her children the mommy who had stopped loving their daddy and banished him from their lives and smashed up their home. She did not want to be the woman who spoke out at school about the sanctity of marriage, and then expose herself as nothing more than a woman driven by lust, who had declared being sweaty on her back in bed as the single most important value in her life. She had to live in this town. You did not get to start over, the way people fantasized. You had to drag around your mistakes and vanities and foolishness like Morley's chain.

Of course, she knew that Hugh slept with all kinds of women and had done so, she suspected, from the second year of their marriage. The shock had been debilitating at first, and then there were years of rages, threats and promises, but nothing ever changed. Sometimes women would call the house, sometimes their *husbands* called the house and demanded to know what they were going to do about the fact that his wife and her husband were sleeping together. Sometimes she found phone numbers in Hugh's jacket pocket that, when she called them, were answered by women sounding expectant and hopeful. And on and on.

But she had children to raise. She needed to be home for them. She did not want to be a single working mother who saw her kids an hour a night. And apart from not loving her — though he insisted he did — Hugh was not cruel or abusive or ungenerous. When they would have dinner out with another couple — usually a work associate of his — she would register, in an abstract sort of way, that she liked him, that his sense of humor amused her, that he was interesting and decent . . . and yet he was incapable of fidelity. Her anger stopped being an active thing; she simply iced over. And then they stopped making love. It had been years and years, not since Craig was a baby. And after the sex stopped, he seemed to not know of any way at all to connect with her.

For her to go to Jim as his wife, he would need to do something more than ask. She was not capable of simply, one afternoon, making a measured decision to wreck her life. Jim would have to march up to the house ring the bell and deck Hugh right there at the front door. Because such an act would be irrevocable, and irreparable, and there would be no choice but to change. But of course, Jim would never ever do such a thing. She doubted he was even capable of imagining it. And she could hardly suggest it to him. He would think she'd lost her mind, and besides, she would not want it to happen by script. It would have to be spon- taneous, like a force of nature, Jim's nature. Even if such a thought had crossed Jim's reasonable mind, he would strenuously repress it. Partly because he did not believe he should have to fight a man Donna herself told him she did not love, and partly because he had his own fantasies about them, didn't he? That she would come to him freely, calmly, with her eyes wide open, that she would not have to be dragged or cajoled. That was Jim's idea of her proving that she loved him. And so they were stuck.

She loaded the dishwasher with breakfast dishes, hers and the kids', and headed up to Carly's room. It was a small, sweet room; she had not, like a lot of teenagers, turned it into some weird shrine to rock bands and shallow celebrities. Yes, she had a stack of CDs by groups Donna objected to. And yes, her closet was a mess of clothes that Donna was mostly disheartened to see her wearing — ugly, oversized things, or cheap, clingy things. But the bedspread was still the sweetheart rose pattern Donna had picked out three years ago, and the bookshelves still had as many stuffed toys as books. Her small desk was neat and organized, a beacon to what was still best about Carly: her essential seriousness and conscientiousness. If she didn't let the other stuff bog her down, she would do well in life. Donna felt fairly sure of this, and it was the one thing that saved her from real panic even in light of Carly's current behavior.

She scanned the bookshelves. She had no good idea what she was looking for. Drugs? Contraceptives? Love letters? Mostly she was looking for a way *in*, some secret map to Carly's psyche that would allow her to help her in a way that Carly wasn't letting her help now. She opened the desk drawers and pushed things around in her closet. She lifted the mattress and peered under the bed. Nothing out of the ordinary or incriminating there. She sat on the bed and nearly gave up. But then, on some instinct, she went back to the closet. She stood on the step stool that was half covered with tossed shoes and scanned the top shelf. There was a cardboard storage box in the far corner. She pulled it down; it was heavy and unwieldy. She settled on the bed with it. Photos, old jewelry, strange keepsakes she could barely identify — was this a popsicle stick? A broken hair brush? And then, clearly, diaries. Two volumes.

She opened them — pages and pages of Carly's handwriting. Her heart was thumping, and it hurt to breathe. Just an adrenaline rush, she told herself, putting her hand on her heart and shutting her eyes. Calm down. *You are her mother, and you are going to do what's best for her.*

She started from the beginning and began to read.

...17

After Natalie died, Lela had not felt saved. That was how everyone else had acted, but she instead had felt sentenced to life. She had practiced thinking of nothing, forcing her mind blank, trying for the oblivion Natalie had talked about. People kept telling her they loved her, but she didn't want any part of it. She was no good at love — what further proof did they need? She didn't deserve to be loved; she was unworthy of it, unequal to it. Her own love was paltry, ineffectual. It was not salvation enough.

She had deserved to die, and once Natalie was gone, she suddenly had the taste for it, the courage for it, but it was too late. Too late because they were all watching her every second, but also because Lela was afraid that if she died then, spaced apart in time from Natalie's, they wouldn't be able to find each other in eternity. That they were separated forever was unfathomable.

Her family had moved. *Of course we have to*, her parents had said. Because it was terrible for them. The talk. The blame. The speculation. Someone said *lesbians*. Her mother acted as though that was worse than Natalie's being dead. They didn't seem to have the additional stamina to address that, too. They went only a couple of counties over, but it might as well have been the other side of the globe. Except that they still occasionally saw sports news about St. Ignatius in the local papers, about the basketball team that didn't go on to victory without Natalie. "The tragic death of star player Natalie Sheehan . . ." the papers would write. No one said *suicide,* at least not in public, as if the whole thing were less obscene with different terminology. As if the *word* would upset Lela, as if she hadn't, for God's sake, been there, been uselessly there, neither able to save nor join her.

They sent her to counseling. She said nothing. She was mute — didn't they know? She would never have anything to say again, because it couldn't be to Natalie. She was deaf, because there would never be any words to hear again from Natalie. There were offers of pills, but she objected to them with rages. What were they treating her for, anyway? What was their idea of the appropriate response to what had happened to her and Natalie? The psychiatrists finally told her parents that her anger was healthy.

She *was* angry. Angry at Natalie's mother and the school and everyone within shouting distance for not making Natalie feel safe, for persecuting her overtly and covertly. At Natalie herself: the stupid, stubborn, selfish, impatient fool. At herself: for cowardice, for failure of spirit, will, and powers of persuasion, for insufficient lovablility that would have been enough to make Natalie stay.

She lived in a barbed cocoon of pain, sharp edges at

every flex, so constant that it became unremarkable. So when, after months and months, she felt something like pleasure occasionally flicker — watching Mr. Biscuits play with his catnip ball — it genuinely surprised her. But even this, meager as it was, was possible only squeezed into small spaces, bookended by the memory of grief on one side and the certainty of its return on the other.

She had graduated from her new high school, went across the country to college under protest from her parents who wanted to keep her like a bird in a cage. She drank more than she ever thought she would, slept with women, each one only a few times before she forgot their names, never wanted to see them again, especially the ones who fell in love with her. They scared the sweat right out of her, they enraged her, for what they were asking her to feel. No one would ever put her through that again. Some of them cursed her, charged her with running from her sexuality, with being closeted, and she wished it were that simple.

By grad school, it had calcified, like lava cooled over a landscape of perfectly preserved horrors. Mostly inactive, able to be viewed with some objectivity. Able to be negotiated.

...18

"Ms. Johns, I've got to talk to you," Carly said breathlessly as she fell into step alongside Lela, who was making her way down the hall to the school's front door.

"What is it?" Lela said, shoving open the swinging door. Students were swarming by them; the last class for the day had just let out. Nearly a week had gone by since the night Lela drove Carly home, and all had been quiet. She supposed she had been naïve to think that might be the end of it.

"Let's wait till no one can hear us," Carly said, her voice brittle. Her complexion looked gray even in the bright sunlight. A stab of fear lodged in Lela's gut, and she picked up her pace as she headed to her car. By the time they got there, Carly had started to cry.

"Get in," Lela said, glancing around, worried about who might be watching this unfold. She pulled out of the parking lot, resisting the impulse to speed. "Carly, what in God's name is wrong?"

"I'm so sorry, Ms. Johns. I've bothered you way too much already, and you've been so nice, and now *this*," Carly said in a kind of hiccup. "I mean, I can't even begin to tell you how sorry I am." She collapsed into tears again, her face pressed into her hands.

"There are tissues in the glove compartment," Lela commanded, fighting back a rising panic. Carly blew her way through three tissues in a row, then stuffed the whole soggy mess into one of her overall pockets.

"My mother," Carly managed finally, "found my diaries."

Lela, her throat closing, decided to head for the supermarket parking lot. The last thing she needed was to get into an accident with a student in the car. In the lot, they could sit fairly innocently and undisturbed.

"What was in there, Carly?" Lela asked after she pulled into a spot by the chain link fence and shut the car off. She left her window cracked so a cool breeze could circulate.

"Well, *everything!* What would you *expect?*" Carly shouted. "That's what a diary is for! It's supposed to be private — no one was ever supposed to read it. I had it hidden and she ransacked my room! I just *hate* her!"

Lela felt a wave of nausea and yanked the visor down against the sun. "What did she read, Carly?" she asked, her voice sounding dead even to her own ears.

Carly bit her bottom lip while her chin quivered. She stared straight ahead at the supermarket dumpster. "Everything. About Fran. About being in love with her and . . . and the stuff we did in bed . . . and how I think I might be queer."

Lela swallowed. That must have knocked Mrs. Matson for a loop. It was one thing to hear your child announce that she was a lesbian. It was another to have to confront it in the purple language of adolescent lust. But it served the woman right, didn't it?

"Of course, she called Fran's mother last night," Carly went on. "I don't even know what they talked about exactly — and Fran didn't come in today. I've been calling during every class break, but there's no answer."

"What else, Carly?"

"I swear to God, I never thought! I feel so terrible I wish I could kill myself!"

"*Hey,*" Lela said, grabbing Carly roughly by the arm. "Don't *ever* say or think crap like that, you hear me?"

Carly was startled sober. "Oh, I, I didn't mean —"

"Nothing is worth that, you understand? *Nothing.*"

"Yes, I —" she said, dragging the back of her hand under her nose.

"Now, what else was in there, Carly?"

She hung her head, and Lela strained to hear her. "Stuff about you. About how you'd been nice to me, heard me out. How you gave me that phone number."

"Oh God, oh God," Lela said, covering her mouth.

This started Carly sobbing again. "I *had* to tell you. I didn't want to. She was an animal. I've never seen her like that. I don't know what she's going to do, but it's going to be bad. I think she's going to tell the school board."

"Well, of course she is," Lela said. "I'm surprised I got through the day's classes. This happened last night?"

Carly nodded. "Can she have you kicked out?"

"Let's not worry about that right now," Lela said, wiping sweat from her upper lip. "Tell me exactly what you said in the diary about my giving you the number. Exactly!"

"I, I can't remember exactly. I mean, she's got the diaries now — it's not like I can check."

"Remember!"

"Uh, for one thing, I taped the little piece of paper you gave me in there. Because it was in your handwriting."

Lela shut her eyes and her head began to spin. She

106

should turn the car around right now and just quit. She felt a kind of numbness setting in, and she wondered if she was going to pass out. This was a new frontier of fear. And yet she had to make sure Carly didn't sense that. "Did you write about coming to my house last weekend?"

"Uh huh. But I hardly said anything about it! Just that I had fought with Fran and they dropped me off there and you drove me home so I wouldn't have to take a cab."

"You're sure?"

"Uh huh."

That *was* all that had happened, Lela reminded herself. It would be hard to twist it into something more. Hard but not impossible, of course. Someone could argue that Lela should have called Carly's parents, she supposed, but not having done that was hardly a hanging offense, was it? It was the damn phone number that could tie the noose. How in the world was she going to defend herself?

Lela opened the car door and swung her legs outside. She leaned forward, hoping to stem the nausea enough to drive. Behind her, she could hear Carly crying. It was terrible that Carly had to see her like this — she had to pull herself together. She settled back into her seat and shut the car door again. "Carly, look. Whatever happens, it's not your fault. You had a right to think your diary was private."

Carly was taking hard breaths. "But I should have hidden it better or something —"

"No, your mother was obviously determined to find something, and she did. You're allowed to live your life. I'm an adult. I take full responsibility for having given you that number." Lela leaned her head back. "Ironic. I did it so I wouldn't have to get involved."

"I'll defend you, Ms. Johns! I'll tell them the truth! I was asking you to help me, and you did! Isn't that was a teacher is *supposed* to do?"

"Well, the school has a different idea of help, Carly, when the situation is that a student thinks she's a lesbian."

"I know. They think I'm sick. My mother said so. She has

a shrink all picked out. But you never thought that, did you?" Carly asked. She was whispering, as in a confessional.

"Carly, we can't be seen together. Not now especially. It'll only make things worse. I have to get you to the bus stop right away." Lela pulled out. "But you have to listen to me — you didn't do anything wrong! And what you feel for Fran — whether or not Fran is the right one for you — don't let them tell you that you don't have a right to your feelings." Lela was practically breathless, trying to cram a lifetime's worth of advice into five minutes. She had no idea when she'd ever get to talk to Carly alone again. Tears stung her eyes. She took an extra loop around the block so she could say more. "What's going to happen, whatever it is, is about adults fighting. It's about politics, you understand? And they're going to say things about me that may scare you and confuse you, and you have to remember who is saying them, always. Try to keep in mind that it may be lies, or it may be only partly true or twisted somehow." She stopped the car at the curb. "You're a brave and strong girl, Carly, with a lot of love to give, and you have a right to live the life you want."

Carly was crying again, and Lela saw the bus turning the corner. A powerful sorrow and regret descended, and she wondered suddenly if it would ever leave.

"Ms. Johns, I —"

"That's your bus, Carly. Just do as I say and get on it."

Carly stumbled out of the car and stood there, as if uncertain how to walk. One of the girls climbing onto the bus spotted her and called her name. Carly turned, and Lela swung her car out into traffic, unwilling to watch the girl slowly recede from view.

...19

"Tell me you're kidding," Jim Fallon said across the table. He and Donna were at a restaurant at the shore, a good half-hour from school. Ever since Carly had hurled her accusation, Donna had insisted on being more careful, and that was just fine by him. He was hoping it would force Donna to take their affair more seriously. "Look, I understand that everything you read in Carly's diary is a shock — Jesus, in love with another girl! I didn't see that coming. But to haul Lela Johns in front of the school board? Based on that asinine new code? You can't have thought this through, Donna."

She fixed him with an icy stare. "I absolutely have

thought this through, Jim. Don't talk to me like I'm one of your slow students."

"You're talking about ruining someone's career!"

"We're talking about ruining my daughter's life!"

"Excuse me, did I miss something? By giving her a phone number?"

"Jim, I'm surprised at you. There's a lot more going on here than a phone number. Maybe you don't see that because you're not a parent. "

Direct hit. All the while she'd been turning down his marriage proposals, he wondered how long it was going to take her to throw in his face that he had no experience at parenting. "You know, I may not be a father myself, but I think I should get a little credit for knowing something about kids, having spent the last fifteen years teaching them —"

"You can stand behind a desk for the next one hundred years, Jim. It's nothing like raising your own child."

He sat back and surveyed the scene from the porch of the old Victorian where they were seated. It was a glorious spring day — the air was sweet, so sweet it was hard to imagine it was ever better, even at the beginning of time. He didn't want to argue on such a beautiful day, but if they were going to argue, he wanted it to at least be about the topic at hand. "Look, all I'm saying is, why don't we address this question of Carly's sexuality, but leave Lela Johns out of it? Carly was obviously casting around for some guidance, and Lela tried to do the least intrusive thing possible, is how it looks to me."

"Jim," Donna said, leaning forward, anger twisting her lips, "what Lela Johns should have done was come to me immediately. Or at least tell Carly to come to me. Instead, she gives her the number of some gay youth group? She might as well have driven her to a gay sex orgy herself!"

Jim coughed up the gulp of coffee he'd just taken. "Donna! Really, you are wildly overreacting!"

"Oh, you think so? I most certainly do not. What do you make of that cozy scene in her apartment? This grown woman, this adult, lets Carly into her home close to midnight, past her curfew, and they compare notes about lesbian lifestyles —"

"Wait a minute — what do you mean, compare notes? What are you insinuating?"

"Stop shouting! People are looking!" Donna sighed. "Jim, really, think about it. What did Carly know about Lela Johns that she felt free to go to her in the first place with such talk?"

"Donna —"

"Hear me out. Carly wrote that she got to Lela Johns' place, she'd had too much to drink —"

"She obviously got shit-faced at the bar, for God's sake!"

"— there are references to this woman's velvet couches and Lela Johns' being sweet to her and swearing Carly to secrecy."

"For the love of God, Donna, you really think Lela Johns decided to ply with alcohol a sixteen-year-old girl who turns up on her doorstep, sweet-talk her and seduce her on the couch!"

"*Stop.* I don't even want to *hear* that kind of talk!"

"But you're the one who imagined it, Donna! You're the one who just painted the scene!"

"All I can tell you for sure is that I've already read the diary passages to a lawyer, and he certainly had some ideas." She pulled a small notebook out of her purse and began to consult it. "If she *did* lay a hand on Carly, there's involuntary deviate sexual intercourse, indecent assault and corruption of the morals of a minor. Even if she *never* laid a hand on her, there's 'false imprisonment' for keeping Carly in the apartment that night past her curfew. There's 'intentional infliction of emotional distress,' which means Lela Johns doing something she knows will hurt Carly. There's something called 'negligent infliction of emotional distress,' which applies to me in this case, for the upset this has caused me. There's 'alienation of affections' and 'loss of consortium,' in that Carly has been lured away from confiding in her family. Some of these are criminal, and some are civil. Some would mean she owes financial damages, some mean jail time. So Lela Johns could be looking at a lot worse than losing her job."

"You're going to get her *arrested?*"

Donna sipped her coffee with a quaking hand. "No, I'm not, actually. It would require too much of Carly, having to be questioned endlessly by lawyers. It's not healthy to have her dwelling on the subject that long. I want this over with as fast as possible."

"Then what are you doing calling a lawyer?"

"For backup. Against exactly the kind of liberal reaction you're having. To show everyone who listens that this is serious enough that there is the law of the land beyond even the law of the school. If you ask me, Lela Johns will be getting off easy if all that happens to her is that she loses her job at Franklin."

Jim's legs began to tremble under the table as he watched Donna. It was a terrible moment. He loved her, as much as ever, but she had just revealed herself to be, in some important way, a stranger, and someone he didn't like at all. How could he have spent this much time with her and still be sucker-punched this way? Was the difference really that piece that was parenthood? Did it make some women literally insane with protectiveness? Like the cases when mothers shoot the cheerleading coach if their daughters don't make the squad. Because this was a staggering display of hysteria on Donna's part, and he'd had not one clue before that she was capable of it.

"What does Carly say about all of this?"

"Well, you can imagine. I'm evil incarnate. She screamed and cried for hours, refused to listen to a shred of reason and is basically not talking to me."

"Donna, forget about Lela Johns. Focus on your daughter now."

"Jim, I have to tell you, I'm shocked that you don't agree with me. I didn't imagine that you'd be one of the people I'd

112

have to fight on this. I thought you were growing to love Carly, and you would be as outraged by what I found as I am."

"I am — I mean, what I mean is, you know how much I care about Carly. And she's clearly in a crisis of some proportion, and we have to help her. But I wish we had known without pillaging her diaries."

"*How dare you*," she said, so coldly he barely recognized her voice. "I would do anything to keep Carly safe, whatever it takes in the short run to protect her in the long run. If I'd stood by and respected her privacy," she said, sneering, "I'd have turned the whole thing over to Lela Johns, wouldn't I? The whole question of Carly's sexual orientation, as you're supposed to call it today. A woman with God knows what motives."

Jim rubbed his temples hard with both hands. This whole conversation was rigged with land mines. "Look, can we try to separate out the issues, here? Let's start with Lela Johns and whether you report her to the school board for violating that crazy code. I have to tell you, Donna, as a teacher myself, I think it sucks. You know, we get emotionally caught up with the kids to some extent. We're decent people and we try to do what's best for them. I've had situations myself where boys have come to me, and their girlfriends are pregnant. And yes, I've given them phone numbers. And I haven't called the parents." He saw that Donna was shaken. "Because it's not my job to be the police, or to mediate between the kids and the parents. I have to make a tough call about whether this boy is old enough to make his own decisions."

"But he's not, Jim — that's the whole point. If you've really done that, it's wrong. It's wrong that you locked the parents out."

"The kid *already* locked the parents out — don't you see? All I did was give a desperate kid some information. I didn't drive him to a clinic."

"You're splitting hairs, Jim. And what if the kid wanted drugs, because he was old enough to make his own decisions?"

"That's absurd. I'm not helping kids hurt themselves, for God's sake!"

"Well, plenty of parents think abortion is wrong, and they don't expect their teachers — whose salaries they pay — to dispense addresses for them! You don't get to decide the moral code that applies."

He was scared now. She had the kind of argument that was going to convince parents. "All right, let's not wade into other controversies, then. Let's stick to this one. You haven't even considered the possibility, have you, Donna, that maybe Carly *is* a lesbian? That maybe it was part of her code since birth and there's nothing you can do about it now but make her feel miserable about what is natural for her — or not. You're content to have the woman who may have been the only buffer between her and despair be crucified in front of the whole community? And then what? Carly is still gay, maybe. And your relationship with your daughter is in tatters."

"Don't try to scare me, Jim. I'm her mother. What kind of mother would I be if I worried she wouldn't like me just because I was doing was what the best possible thing for her, which is to protect her from the perverted impulses of adults who have no conscience. Not to mention those of peers, too! I never liked that Fran character she was hanging around with. I swear, I could ring her neck when I think of what she has started Carly on."

"Are you going to bring us all up to the school board, Donna? All the teachers for everything we ever said to a student that we didn't run by her parents first? Why not sue everyone who advertises to kids, and TV networks, too? The world is a big place — there's a lot of blame to go around. Why stop with such small potatoes like a bunch of teachers?"

"Sarcasm doesn't become you, Jim. Leave it to Hugh."

"Ah, Hugh. Which brings us to another interesting

dilemma. Forget the fireworks you'll make in front of the school board — and you will, you must know that. The press'll love to get a hold of this kind of thing. What about in your heart of hearts? How do you sit in judgment of your daughter's life, your daughter's choice of lovers, when you yourself —"

"Stop it! That's sick! It's not the same at all. You and I," she hissed across the table, "are adults. Consenting adults. I'm not proud of being an adulterer. You don't know how close I've come to never seeing you again, Jim. Does that scare you? It scared me, but I'd do it if I really had to to save my daughter. But Carly is a sixteen-year-old girl. She doesn't know yet what her life should be. My God, she's declaring she's a lesbian and she hasn't even slept with a boy! And she's got this teacher who's a one-woman cheerleader for the lesbian lifestyle. How can you say that's anything at all like an adult man and an adult woman who realize they're in the wrong marriages?"

He held his breath and felt his eyes well. "Is that you, Donna. In the wrong marriage?"

She lowered her eyes. "Maybe, Jim, when this whole thing is over, when Carly is off at college . . ."

It was a devil's bargain, he knew. And he was ashamed of himself for making it. Stand by the woman he loved now, even though in every fiber of his soul he thought she was wrong, and maybe she would be his one day. Because, he was sure, when that one day came, he would still want her.

...20

Lela had just shown Kit the neatly typed letter, with the school district's name and address printed at the tip, which read: *Please report to a private school board hearing on April 30th at 4 p.m.* It didn't say much else, but it didn't have to. Lela knew exactly what it meant.

Kit was stomping around the living room. "It's just outrageous!" she was saying. "It's *stupid*. I mean, what can they possibly say? You haven't done anything wrong."

Lela smiled grimly. "My union rep didn't think so. I could hear her suck in her breath when I told her I had given Carly the number of a gay youth group — and the kid taped it into her diary for proof."

"It wasn't like that —"

"I know what it was like, Kit. For God's sake, *I* know what it was like."

"I'm sorry, I —"

"Well, get over the idea that the world is fair."

Kit stopped pacing and stared. Her oversized T-shirt hung down to the middle of her thighs, and her hair was sticking up oddly from having run her hands over it every which way. "You know, you're scaring me. I feel like you're going to go in there tomorrow and roll over and let them say and do whatever they want."

"They're going to say and do whatever they want anyway, whether I roll over, or sit up and beg."

"Is that what the union rep thinks, too? Is she any good, do you know?"

"Her name is Rita Sinclair. She seems pretty standard issue to me, but what do I know? I haven't had much experience being called before the school board."

Kit sat down; she finally seemed worn out. Perched at the edge of the couch, she rubbed the back of her neck. "It doesn't help that you're so new, does it?"

"Rita says they don't even have to have a hearing. They can just dismiss me, with no explanation."

Kit looked up, wide-eyed. "So what does she think it means that they're having a hearing?"

"Two possibilities. One is that they're deciding to cover their butts because it's the kind of charge they think I might sue over."

"Did she really say 'cover their butts'?"

"Yeah, she did." Lela returned Kit's smile.

"Maybe she'll be good, after all. What's the second?"

"That they're looking to make an example of me, that they want it to be a public circus."

"I thought it was a private hearing."

"This one is. But she said not to expect it to be over tomorrow."

"It's just the beginning, then," Kit said, putting her head in her hands.

"You know, I have no idea what they're capable of," Lela said. "If you don't want to get dragged into this, you might want to sever all contact with me starting today."

"When are you going to get it, Lela?" Kit said. "I'd come and stand beside you tomorrow if you'd let me, if you thought it would do any good at all."

The lump that had been lodged in her throat loosened slightly. Maybe she could believe it, the idea that someone would stand beside her, that she didn't have to face everything alone. She allowed herself to submit to Kit's embrace, even as she kept her worst fears to herself.

...21

The school board held its meetings in a civic building downtown, a space big enough to house hundreds of parents when it came time for elections and debates that drew crowds, Rita Sinclair explained to Lela when they met out front at a quarter to four.

"Good outfit," Rita said warmly, and Lela felt relief wash over her. She had agonized about what to wear, and besides, she was eager for good omens. She had settled on a simple tan skirted suit, with a hunter-green scarf tucked inside the neckline. "Let's see, it should be right around this corner," Rita said, pushing her glasses up the bridge of her nose with her knuckle. She was a short, stout woman, and her purple knit dress strained a little across her hips. Her dark hair was piled into waves, a style Lela recognized as popular with her mother's generation. Her gray eyes darted impatiently.

"Have you done this a lot?" Lela asked as Rita yanked open the door and led them into a bland room with yellow cinderblock walls and fluorescent lighting. At the front, there was a podium and two long conference tables set up facing each other some ten feet apart. Rita led them to the one on the left, pulling out chairs for both of them and slapping her files down in front of her.

"Oh, sure. I've been in the union twenty-three years. I've seen a lot. It used to be teachers accused of drinking on the job or ripping off the supply closet. Now I get married men accused of groping their gym students. AIDS cases. Cases like yours."

Lela scanned Rita's face for any flicker of judgment, but she could detect nothing beyond toughness and seriousness of purpose.

"What do we know about the school board?" Lela asked, settling on the insubstantial metal chair. She suddenly felt as though she couldn't get enough air, and her stomach was sloshing with acid.

"Five members. Three women, two men. Long-timers, for the most part, except for one of the women, who got on only last year as a big supporter of the 6540 policy that they're going to try to fit like a noose around your neck."

Lela felt a surge of fear run through her like a current, but there was no time to ask Rita more. From a side door, a cluster of men and women entered, smiling and chatting, and Lela, standing at Rita's nudging, resented them immediately for their casual manner on this day they'd plotted so harshly against her.

"Try not to look like you'd claw their eyes out if only you could get a little closer," Rita muttered to her.

Lela tried to soften her expression, but she suspected she

wasn't successful. "There are more than five people here," she whispered to Rita.

"Parents. Your accusers. They get to come and make their case."

Carly's mother. One of the women had to be Donna Matson, Lela realized. There were five women seated behind the table now, and none of them looked especially like Carly. Only one of the women, dressed in a baby-blue sweat suit with her hair barely contained with a headband, looked conspicuously less professional than the others.

The room quieted down all at once, and the man seated center, fifty-ish and mustached, pushed the microphone away from him. "I don't think we'll need this today, do you, Rita?" he asked, smoothing his plain brown tie.

"No, fortunately, Phil," she said.

"Well, let me introduce everyone, then," he said. "I'm Phillip Ferrante, president, and we have the full school board in attendance — Doug Douglass," he said, gesturing to the blunt-faced, football player-proportioned man to his right, "Lisa MacDonald, Beverly Ferguson and Jamie Walsh." Jamie was the youngest by far, a long-haired blond in her early thirties, Lela guessed, who was probably the one Rita had alluded to as potentially the most troublesome. "We also have with us today two parents, Donna Matson, a PTO member," Phil Ferrante continued, gesturing to the far end of the table, "and Cathy Reilly."

Lela was on overload; she barely heard Rita introducing them or felt her yanking on her sleeve to get her to sit down. Donna Matson was a petite, fine-featured woman, auburn-haired, pretty in her paisley dress. She kept her eyes downcast, and Lela wondered if it was out of guilt or hatred. The bigger shock was that she'd recruited Fran's mother — the one in the sweat suit — to come along. Cathy Reilly reminded Lela of a pumpkin: ruddy complexioned, with bulging cheeks and wide, startled eyes.

"Phil, let me start with a request," Rita was saying when

Lela was able to force her attention back. "Lela Johns has been given extremely limited notice of this hearing, and she has not been told in any way, shape or form what the allegations are. Rather than prolong this unnecessarily, I'm not asking that we reconvene at a later date, but that you simply allow us an hour to privately review the specific accusations before we answer them."

"You know, Rita," Phil said, "we considered that, but given the urgency of the matter, and the straightforwardness of the circumstances, we felt unanimously that this was the best way to proceed."

Lela saw Rita's lips purse into a thin, straight line. "Well, then," she said, "please let the meeting minutes reflect that." Beverly Ferguson, the only black member, dutifully scribbled on a legal pad.

"All right," Phil said, vigorously rubbing his jaw. "I will let Mrs. Matson present the circumstances."

"Yes, thank you, Phil," Donna Matson said, nodding at him from her end of the table. When she looked up, she didn't let her eyes so much as flicker on Lela; she addressed her comments to Rita as she read from a sheet of paper. "Lela Johns, during one of many after-class sessions she sought with my daughter, Carly Matson, gave her, and her friend Fran Reilly, the name and phone number of a local 'gay youth' group, whose express purpose is to support and encourage teenagers in the homosexual lifestyle. This group freely gave out the location of a local gay bar and encouraged both girls to go. They did, on the night of April twelfth, and were allowed entrance, although they are five years under the legal drinking age. Further," Donna Matson continued, her voice growing thinner, "on the same night of April twelfth, after having left the gay bar, Carly was invited into Lela Johns' home and kept there past her curfew. Lela Johns served alcohol and counseled my daughter on how to achieve happiness in a lesbian lifestyle."

"This is *insane!*" Lela shouted, leaping out of her chair.

"Calm down," Rita whispered harshly, giving Lela's forearm a death grip.

But she couldn't. She felt assaulted to the core. She could no more calm herself than she could have stood still while someone struck her with blows. "I've never heard such unadulterated, baseless hogwash in my life!" Lela shouted, never once taking her eyes off Donna Matson, who now, finally, coldly returned her gaze. "How can you sit there and sling such slander around!"

"Phil, Phil, really, you see," Rita shouted over Lela's shouting, "it simply is unfair not to give a person time to prepare herself. This comes as a shock. And frankly I think it points to her innocence as well as passion for the truth —"

"It does no such thing," Donna Matson shot back as the others fidgeted with apparent embarrassment and alarm.

"Ms. Johns, you will get a grip on yourself and behave accordingly," Phil said.

"What's the proper way to behave, Mr. Ferrante," Lela said, her voice raspy with scorn, "when someone is trying to wreck your reputation with lies and accusations that are reprehensible to you?"

"That's what we're here to discuss. Now settle down. You can rebut these charges in due time — if you do so civilly."

Lela gripped the edge of the table. Why should she be civil, she wanted to ask, when this whole proceeding was barbaric? She and Rita had in fact rehearsed some possible responses, assuming the gay youth phone number was the point, but neither of them had been able to guess that Donna Matson would have twisted the late-night visit this perversely out of shape.

"Mrs. Matson," asked Phil Ferrante, "were you finished?"

"Not quite. I was about to say that Lela Johns then swore Carly Matson to secrecy about their assignation. We have the unusual benefit of proof in that all this has been recorded in my daughter's diary —" Donna Matson held the little notebook up — "which she offered to me recently when she became uncomfortable with the counsel she was being given by Ms. Johns, and asked that I help her sort through her feelings and confusion."

Lela felt outraged to the point of violence, but this time she stayed quiet till she was sure Donna Matson was through.

"In conclusion, these are all behaviors explicitly in violation of Policy 6540, which, as we all know, forbids teachers to initiate discussion of homosexuality in classes or in clubs, or to make any remarks or take any action that could be construed to be supportive or encouraging of homo- sexuality. It seems clear to me and Mrs. Reilly that this policy is tailor-made to protect students and their families in cases like ours, and I implore the school board to act as forcefully and quickly as possible, for the good of all Franklin students."

Out of the corner of her eye, Lela saw Rita Sinclair lean back in her chair, but whether it was out of defeat or disbelief, she couldn't tell.

"Lela Johns, you may speak now in your defense."

Where should she begin? She hardly knew. Was there time to present the entire history of homophobia throughout civilization? Probably not. "First I'd like to ask a question," Lela said. "The girls themselves, both students in my English class, can tell you that nothing happened the way Mrs. Matson claims it did. Carly Matson turned up on my doorstep about eleven thirty one night, uninvited, completely to my surprise and displeasure, which I made clear. She told me her curfew was midnight. Rather than entrust her to a cab at that time of night and have her risk missing her curfew, I promptly bundled her up and drove her home. Why can't Carly be here to say for herself what happened?"

Rita kicked Lela's shoe under the table, a warning, no doubt, to keep the sneer out of her voice. "Ms. Johns," said Lisa MacDonald, wearing a shower of brightly colored beads over her red cotton shirt-dress, "I asked that myself, but of course we can't expect the girls to incriminate themselves. Even if they refuted Donna Matson's version, it doesn't prove anything to me."

"By the same token, it doesn't prove anything that Donna Matson said these things happened, either," Lela said, exasperated.

"If you are saying Carly will be intimidated by her mother and not tell the whole truth," Lisa MacDonald said, "how do I know she won't be similarly intimated by you?"

"More to the point, Ms. Johns," Jamie Walsh interrupted, "let me remind you that it is *you*, granted the privilege of being a teacher in this school district, who is being called here to explain yourself. No one on this podium is obliged to defend herself or himself to you. What's more, I've heard you say nothing so far about the matter of having given the girls the name and phone number of a gay youth group."

"I don't deny that," Lela said, giving herself over to a small shudder. This was one of the answers she had rehearsed with Rita. "I knew it was in violation of the policy, and I regretted that. But I felt that this was a mature and stable student who had repeatedly asked me for information in this area. I made it clear that my giving her the number was not an endorsement, and I strongly encouraged her to talk to her family and school counselors in addition."

"And how did you come to know this number in the first place?" Jamie Walsh asked.

"I simply called Information."

"So you clearly gave this thought and deliberation — this notion of figuring out how to help a sixteen-year-old girl pursue and embrace her lesbian sexual identity?" Jamie asked.

Hopelessness fell around Lela's shoulders like a lead blanket. She saw the school board before her in one snapshot — well-dressed, middle-class, heterosexual parents protecting the virtue of their children. Even if she were to prove beyond the shadow of a doubt that that night at her apartment was as innocent as she knew it to be, she herself would still be a lesbian, and wasn't that what they all suspected and were really out to prove? She heard the first thin whistle of the approaching train on the tracks.

"May I speak here, please?" Rita said. "The business of the

phone number aside for a moment, there is nothing in Lela John's record to indicate that she was doing anything more than helping a student in a jam one night, at considerable inconvenience to herself, which this hearing is no small demonstration of. She simply brought Carly Matson home safely, for which she should be commended, not punished."

"Your version of Lela Johns as savior is premature," Jamie Walsh said, obviously just warming up, Lela saw. "First let's have her convince me that she did not arrange ahead of time a rendezvous with a minor girl at her apartment, after having played a role in getting that minor girl to a homosexual bar that very night, with the express purpose of demonstrating to this girl that a homosexual lifestyle was acceptable and fun, and perhaps one she shared herself."

"Ex*cuse* me!" Rita's voice rose an octave. "Just what are —"

"And besides," Cathy Reilly jumped in, "Franny told me that she wanted to take Carly straight home, but Carly made it plain that she had business alone with this teacher at her apartment."

"These are reckless, slanderous accusations!" Rita shouted.

Lela covered her face with her hands, trying by force of will to stop the train racing for her on its tracks.

"Ms. Johns, do you have a boyfriend or a fiancé who can attest to your moral character in this regard?" Jamie Walsh asked.

Rita was on her feet now. "Look, if Lela Johns is being accused of more than driving a girl home, then what you're hinting at is a criminal charge and she has a right to a lawyer, and you're going to need something in the way of real evidence."

"Settle down, everyone," Phil Ferrante said. "It's not going to come to that today, Rita. My recommendation is to put a full report of this in Ms. John's personnel file —"

"It doesn't *belong* in my file. You have no *grounds*!" Lela said.

"Well, you can take that up with the superintendent of

schools, if you like, Ms. Johns, but this board feels unanimously that this incident belongs in your file, and you are officially placed on probation for the rest of the semester. Are we agreed on this point, members of hte school board?"

They all murmured their consent.

"Given the fact that you don't dispute the basic allegation, Ms. Johns," Phil continued, "that you in fact gave a student the phone number of a gay youth group and that you entertained her for some brief period past her curfew in your apartment without having notified her parents, I do think this is the only responsible course of action for us."

"Look, I was found in a burning building and you're saying you can tell from the face of it that I was the person who started the fire."

"That's a lovely metaphor, Ms. Johns, but you can save those for your English classes," Jamie Walsh said. "Teachers are held to a higher standard for the good of the whole community, and its most malleable members."

"And it will remain in your file," Phil went on, reading from a document, "with a warning to, in general, exhibit better judgment as regards your students, and specifically to strictly adhere to school policy 6540 on the matter of homosexuality, and to have no outside class conversations or communication of any kind with Carly Matson and Fran Reilly, and no private meetings with any girl students on school premises or off unless prearranged so that another teacher can be present. If you have faithfully adhered to these directions in every detail by the end of the school year, we will consider a petition from you to have this warning removed and these restrictions lifted."

"This is outrageous!" Lela said.

"Are we agreed on this?" Phil Ferrante asked his board.

"I'm not persuaded, Phil," Jamie Walsh said. Lela felt she was trying to aim her righteous voice at her as though it were a weapon. "Frankly, I see cause for suspension right now. I find that Ms. Johns is argumentative, disrespectful, uncooperative and without remorse. Further, she freely admits she consciously acted in violation of Policy 6540, and I see no reason to think she won't do so again, perhaps with even more disastrous results. All this leaves me uneasy that the worst of the charges could very well be true, and that all the female students at Franklin could potentially be at risk."

"Do I have a second to that from another board member?" Phil asked, glancing to his right and left. They all looked down at the their hands. "No, you don't have a second on that today, Jamie, but Ms. Johns, I will repeat to you that these are serious charges indeed and you will be monitored closely and judged less generously should there be any other complaint this semester."

A collective scraping of chairs followed, and the seven of them marched off the podium and back out the door they came in.

Rita sat slumped, shaking her head. "I'm sorry," she said mournfully.

But Lela was relishing a victory she couldn't share — she had managed to stave off an attack; the terror had not overtaken her. Maybe there would be a way to live with Natalie's memory instead of reliving the agonies of her death. Maybe she had run far enough, maybe she could be free. Maybe.

...22

Lela had been sitting in her car across the street from Natalie Sheehan's house for close to an hour. In many ways, the block and the neighborhood, looked stuck in time: the modest brick houses, the wide streets, the intersections busy with housewives out shopping and dragging children by the hands. But now the families had minivans and SUVs instead of station wagons, and in the backyards there were brightly colored plastic play gyms instead of the wood and steel swing sets Lela remembered.

Lela had watched a woman enter the Sheehan house a little while earlier, a woman who by height, apparent age and sensible, shapeless nurse's shoes could have been Natalie's mother. But Lela wasn't be sure. The Sheehans might have moved or rented the house, or died, even. Lela hadn't kept track. In one way, the rest of the family didn't exist without Natalie; in another, Natalie was so alive in Lela's head she hadn't ever needed anyone else to help conjure her.

Lela kept staring at the house, at the front door, the upstairs windows, behind which was Natalie's old room, where they had spent so many late afternoons into dusk. If there were such things as ghosts, Lela imagined that Natalie's would live there, in that bed where they had lain, and kissed and touched.

It was wrong, Lela felt, to just show up after ten years, to still be alive. She had hid, she knew, because she imagined the very fact of her life would be an affront to Mrs. Sheehan. She couldn't imagine getting out of the car and just walking across the street to that front door. It was as if there was a force field between her and the house, and she was not strong enough to overcome it. She should have at least called first; it went against her sense of manners not to, but she didn't dare risk the woman's refusing to see her, or asking her to explain herself fully on the phone.

Not that Lela was sure she could explain in person, either. She couldn't really explain it to herself. All she was clear about was that in order to fight the school board, in order to decide how far she wanted to go to help Carly, in order to figure out if there'd ever be a way to love someone again, in order to go forward with her life in any way that mattered, she needed to understand what had happened between her and Natalie. Needed to understand in a way she hadn't been able to understand by herself, even after all these years.

She slammed the car door shut behind her, feeling hotly con- spicuous. She imagined, as she walked self-consciously across the street, that neighbors' noses were pressed to their windows, and they were whispering, *My God, isn't that the girl who nearly got killed with Natalie Sheehan on the railroad tracks? What's she want with this place after all this time? Come to upset her mother with memories? Wonder if they were a pair of lezzies like everyone said?*

She rang the doorbell, feeling her tongue stick dryly to the roof of her mouth. These were old, solid houses, tall and narrow, with shallow stoops. When the door swung open, and the woman she had just seen on the street pulled the door open, Lela was unprepared. She stared, and saw that they recognized each other. Mrs. Sheehan, with her ruddy cheeks and now slate-gray bob, looked much the same. Those pale blue eyes — Natalie's eyes — were somehow paler, but seeing them now was as close as Lela figured she'd ever get to seeing Natalie alive again. Goose bumps sprouted up along her arms.

"Mrs. Sheehan? I'm, I'm Lela Johns. I don't know if you remember me. I'm sorry I didn't call before coming by."

The older woman tucked her shoulders back. "Lela Johns. You hardly need to say your name. I'd have recognized you anywhere. There hasn't been a day that's gone by that I haven't thought of you and wondered if you were okay."

Tears sprang to Lela's eyes, and in her embarrassment she tried to scowl them away. She had imagined a lot of initial reactions, but none of them was this, something bordering on welcome and sympathy. She had expected to have to explain why she was here at all, not why she hadn't come sooner. But Mrs. Sheehan's manner didn't demand an explanation. She acted as though they were merely continuing a conversation that had gotten badly interrupted.

Mrs. Sheehan held the door open wider, and Lela stepped into the living room. Here was the green and brown area rug she remembered, the felt-striped wallpaper, the corduroy couches, all worse for the wear. Even so, the house looked so much the same that the expectation that Natalie would come loping down the stairs and swing around the corner to greet her was so palpable, so present, that she couldn't take another step.

"I know, it must be a lot, to see the house again," Mrs. Sheehan said, patting Lela's arm and leading her into the dining room. "Come in, sit down. I was just about to have some herb tea. At the hospital these days, everybody swears by it, you know. We have a lot to catch up on."

"Yes, thank you," Lela said, sitting down at the glossy wood dining room table while Mrs. Sheehan opened cabinets in the kitchen. Lela was glad for the few moments alone to acclimate herself. She hadn't anticipated this — how the physical evidence of Natalie's life would hit her with such force. For so long Natalie had been an abstract torment in Lela's mind, and to confront anew the fact of her as a flesh and blood teenage girl whose life had simply ended, while those who loved her had gone on, was a fresh shock.

Across the room was a breakfront, stocked with china and figurines. Lela spotted some picture frames and went over to inspect them. There was Natalie, at about fifteen, in her orange and yellow basketball uniform, sitting on the steps out front, the steps Lela had just walked up, leaning her elbows on her knees and smiling for the camera, her blond hair spilling around her shoulders. Lela felt herself begin to quake all over; she did not have a single picture of Natalie, except for some smeary black and white shots in one of their yearbooks of her rushing down the basketball court. Taking pictures was not the kind of thing fifteen- and sixteen-year-olds thought to do then, not with their whole lives rushing up to greet them every day, and after Natalie died, Lela's family had fled, and there was no time, no way, to ask for one. Not that her parents would have allowed it, anyway. Lela studied the young face now, the long, sinewy legs, and saw that Natalie was both exactly how she remembered her, and not. Years and memory had played their tricks. For one thing, Lela realized she had aged Natalie in her mind's eye, allowed her to grow up, matured her to a strapping young woman in her late twenties. And yet here Natalie was, stopped in time, younger and less forceful than Lela remembered.

"It's a nice shot, isn't it?" Mrs. Sheehan said, startling her. She whirled around to see her carrying two cups filled with a light green steaming broth.

"It is. I, uh, don't have any pictures of her."

"Oh," Mrs. Sheehan said, her expression slack with regret. "That's a real shame. You ought to. I know you loved her, too."

Lela sat back down and stared into the cup with more attention than it deserved. She didn't trust herself to be able to hold it steady. Her heart was swollen up in her throat, cramming out words.

"I mean to say, I know *how* you loved her, and I'm at peace with it, now," Mrs. Sheehan said, taking a delicate sip of tea. Lela dared to look at her, to see if she could mean these astounding things. "Oh, I see what you're thinking. I'm no radical, of course, and if you'd have come here even just five years sooner, I'd have been less sanguine. But ten years is a long time, and it's a longer time for an old woman like me. It's silly to do anything but accept. Natalie was who she was, and one small thing I'm grateful for is that we didn't spend a lot of time fighting specifically about that. But then," she said, laughing, "Natalie gave us so many things to worry about, that seemed the least of it. We suspected, of course, Nick and I —"

"How *is* your husband?" Lela asked, wanting to know if they'd be interrupted by Mr. Sheehan coming in from somewhere.

"Oh," she said, holding up a hand, "Nick died two years after Natalie. If there's such a thing of dying of a broken heart, that's what he did. I believe that. He developed a heart condition not six months after we buried Natalie, and he was never really well again. After he died, my son tried to get me to come live up in Boston with him and his wife, but I wasn't ready to leave. Maybe someday I will, but my job was and is one of the few things I had left that I really took pleasure in. And besides," she said, looking around the room carefully, as if taking some kind of mental inventory, "I felt Natalie's presence here. It was like company. I got over the

feeling that she might come back, just show up, you know —
the whole thing revealed as a big mistake — but I never got
over the feeling that she's still here in some way."

Lela was helpless to stop the tears that slid down her
cheek. "I'm sorry," she croaked, meaning not just about her
husband, but about a thousand things. This was also something she had somehow never managed to contemplate: that
Mrs. Sheehan would be lonely, too, that she would want to
talk, that she was waiting for release, as well. It was astounding, really, how little she had thought of Natalie's mother, and
when she did, it had been only as Natalie had painted her: a
stoic jailer, someone who would stop at nothing to keep
them apart. "How did you . . . come to realize . . . about
Natalie and me?"

Mrs. Sheehan laughed, as if Lela had asked her to tell
some merry family story. There was this, too, then, the possibility of remembering Natalie with joy. "Well, I guess teenagers think their parents are blind nitwits. Natalie fairly
swooned when you were in a room, and I tried as much as I
could to keep you two from ever being alone, but I could
hardly do that except by quitting my job and following her
around all the time, which I couldn't afford to do and keep
this house. There was no point in forbidding Natalie from
seeing you — she was too strong-willed for that. I used to
pray that convention or conscience would keep you both
from doing anything physical, and then maybe it would all
blow over the way lots of school-girl crushes do. But," she
said, smiling and sliding her eyes away, "Natalie had left
behind lots of things she'd written, and they didn't leave
much to the imagination."

"Ah," Lela said, blushing furiously. She shakily lifted the
tea cup, spilling some of it into the saucer but otherwise
getting it safely to her lips.

"So, now that you're here, I don't have to wonder. Tell
me how are you, really. What's brought you here just now?"

"Well, I'm a teacher. In a high school. A couple of
counties over." Lela paused to let this sink in — for Mrs.

Sheehan's sake, but it fell on her own ears in a new way. She felt a tentative stirring of pride. Maybe that *was* who she was, who she deserved to be. "I have some students now who — well, I think I see some of me in them, some of Natalie, and I don't know how to help."

Mrs. Sheehan cradled her cup with her hands, as if against some chill. "You know, one of the things I regretted never getting to tell you, Lela," Mrs. Sheehan said, "was more about Natalie's . . . condition. A mother loves her children, no matter what, but . . ." She frowned into the distance. "But I knew she was a dangerous influence. She may not have told you, but she had made a serious suicide attempt once before. That's why we were so afraid to have her out of the hospital. I didn't feel the doctors had it under control. Her diagnosis was bipolar disorder. Even as a nurse, I hadn't heard much about it. But it's common for it to first show up in adolescence. People who have it have a manic stage where they feel all charged up and ecstatic and go on spending sprees and the like. I used to call these her high spirits. It can also be when they have incredible rages, which Natalie had, too. She had all the symptoms."

Lela remembered Natalie telling her about flinging a picture at her mother, and she flashed on the image of the fabulous gold necklace, and the wild plans to transport them to Amsterdam.

"All the doctors had to offer me," Mrs. Sheehan continued, "was to make sure she took the lithium. They said it took a full two weeks of taking it to have any effect. That's why they agreed to hospitalize her, so we could be sure Natalie would take the pills, and we could see if she responded. But she hated taking them. She said they kept her from feeling happy, and that's apparently part of the manic stage, too. The patients get hooked on that high — they feel like they can do any- thing, they don't see it as problem that needs to be treated. And the lithium did help. She was better, calmer, more even- keeled when she got out. But it wasn't long before she stopped taking the pills. I tried everything —

pleading and threatening. She'd humor me, say she was taking them, would even take a few pills standing in front of me, but I could always tell when she'd stopped." Mrs. Sheehan pressed a trembling hand to her lips.

"Did the nuns at school know?"

"Yes, I told the principal, tried to get the school nurse in on administering the medicine. And they said all the right things, but I could tell they didn't buy it. They thought Natalie was just a willful, stubborn girl who needed more discipline and more religion."

Lela remembered Sister Kathleen's warnings, the judgmental tone of her little soliloquies. "What was the other suicide attempt about?"

"Well, you know, it's not like there was a rational explanation. The doctors said that any life change — simply going into adolescence would count — can trigger an episode. It's possible that the additional stress of realizing she was attracted to other girls was a factor for Natalie. The thing about bipolar disorder is that the flipside is depression. And those spells were just as low as the highs were high. Without the lithium, suicide is a real risk during the depressive stage. I could see how hopeless she was feeling right before . . . you know. She stayed in bed almost that whole spring break, showed no interest in playing basketball, or even talking to you. She wouldn't eat much and lost a lot of weight."

Lela shut her eyes, nearly overcome at the memory of that morning in homeroom, when she saw Natalie after they'd been apart that week. Natalie had looked gaunt, but there was no way she could have known what to make of it. The sense- lessness of it all, the waste, the anguish. They had all been swept up in it, had all suffered alone, islands unto themselves. What might have happened had they all spoken up, all joined hands — the doctors, the school, the Sheehans?

"None of this was clear in the beginning, you understand," Mrs. Sheehan said. "We were all still figuring it out when you first started getting close to Natalie. And sometimes she was fine, even without the pills. It's a very unpredictable illness. When she'd have her normal stretches — well, she was such a rare and lovely person. Playful and joyous and funny, a natural leader — well, *you* know. Everyone loved her. And then, when the episodes came, it was like the best of her left, and all her weaknesses were magnified. And she broke all our hearts not helping herself with the pills." Mrs. Sheehan's eyes welled up.

"It wasn't your fault," Lela said.

"But that's exactly what I wanted to tell *you*, Lela," she said. "I suspected you thought you should have been able to save Natalie that day, but a million strong men couldn't have pulled her to safety if she hadn't wanted to come. Her father and I could have kept her pinned to a wall somewhere, I suppose, like a butterfly on display, but that's not my idea of living, and I know it wasn't hers."

"For a long time," Lela said quietly, slowly, "I felt I should have gone with her."

Mrs. Sheehan reached out and covered Lela's hand with her own. Her skin was cool and dry, and for a moment, it seemed the only sensation in the room. It was powerfully sensual, to be touched by Natalie's mother — blood of her blood, flesh of her flesh — and Lela felt an exquisite terror. "I'm glad you didn't," Mrs. Sheehan said. "Not then, not since. If only for my selfish sake, so as not to have had the two of you on my conscience. Promise me you won't ever think that anymore."

You promised, you promised, you promised.

"I'm not so good at promises, Mrs. Sheehan."

"Well, maybe what you mean is you know the difference between what someone has the right to ask you to promise, and not." The older woman sat back and sighed sadly. "Nick just gave up, you know. That's what did him in. Not that I didn't suffer every bit as much — I did — but he didn't allow himself any quarter at all. I felt we had tried — I *knew* we had tried — to save her. Of course, that newspaper reporter didn't help, either."

"What do you mean?"

"Oh, for a full year after Natalie died, a lady reporter called and wrote, saying she wanted to interview us — and you — to do a follow-up story about what had really happened. To help parents and kids alike, she said. At the time, I just thought she was the worst kind of vulture. I couldn't believe how shameless they were, to go that low to sell papers. Nick took it to mean she wanted to tell people all the ways he was to blame. We never responded." She paused and sipped her tea, staring blankly as if she were alone in the room. "Later on I came to think that maybe she actually meant well. I still read about kids who kill themselves — some on the tracks, too, the very same way — and I think of their poor parents, how they'll live with that pain forever, and I think, I wonder if anything I might have said after the fact would make a difference to anyone."

"Do you remember who the reporter was?"

"Oh, sure. She still writes for the paper. She has her own column now. She comments on this and that, the way they all do these days. Everyone has a soap box. She's done a fair amount lately on gay rights. I think I have a paper around here somewhere." She moved quickly, the way Lela imagined she did at the hospital, streamlined and purposeful. "Yes, here," Mrs. Sheehan said, pulling the paper open and pointing. The column showed a postage-stamp-sized photo of the writer, but it was enough for Lela to guess from it that she was probably a lesbian. Lela gave herself over to a small shiver of the hunted. Had this woman planned to expose her, at sixteen? She committed the name to memory: Ann Ellery. She closed the paper.

"I think you *could* make a difference," Lela said.

"Maybe now," Mrs. Sheehan said. "But not then. Natalie's case was complicated. I see that even more clearly now. This reporter wanted to make pure politics out of it, but Natalie didn't take her life because she was a lesbian — at least I don't think so. She happened to be a gay teenager who happened also to have a mental vulnerability separate from that. But maybe . . . maybe if it had been easier for her to love you openly—" here Mrs. Sheehan stole a shy glance at Lela—"maybe she wouldn't have been so volatile."

Lela sat quietly, awed by the insights Mrs. Sheehan had arrived at over a decade. For herself, she had merely been a prisoner of the same terror, and had done nothing to help herself, or anyone else. If Mrs. Sheehan had made some sense out of losing a beloved daughter, couldn't Lela find some way to peace, too? "I wish you could talk to this one girl's mother in my school, tell her what you just told me," Lela said. "It's not that I think the girl is going to hurt herself, but a lot of people are going to get hurt while this mother tries to stop her daughter from . . . to keep her from . . ."

"Are you one of them? One of the people who's going to get hurt?"

"It's not what you think," Lela said, getting up to pace, suddenly hot all over, imagining that Mrs. Sheehan saw her as someone wreaking havoc wherever she went. "I've tried like anything not to get involved."

"I can see how you would. But you know, I don't believe one mother believes another on this. This woman would just decide *I* had failed *my* daughter, but that doesn't mean she has to fail hers."

"Well, I don't see how *I* can help her."

"No."

"I've been lucky enough to help myself the little I've been able to."

"Yes."

Lela got up and leaned against the doorway into the living room, at the bottom of the stairs.

"Would you like to see Natalie's room?" Mrs. Sheehan asked. "I haven't changed it much."

Lela had a picture of it in her mind, exact enough for her purposes—the window, the desk, the narrow bed pushed into the corner, a bed she nearly always saw unmade. She glanced up the stairs, nearly crushed by longing. How incredible it would be if Natalie were up there, where she'd always found her, pulling her into her arms, giving her those first of first kisses, with their unmatched sweetness and intensity. But up those stairs, all that was left was the obliteration that Natalie wanted as her legacy. Gravity was working too hard on her; she feared her legs would give way. "I think," Lela said, "that I'm not up to it just now. But maybe . . . I mean, if you wouldn't mind . . . if I could come back some other time and visit again . . ."

Mrs. Sheehan got up and stood beside her. "I'd be sorry if you didn't. Wait, take this before you go," she said, turning back to the breakfront and holding out the framed photo of Natalie.

"Oh, no, I couldn't," Lela said, recoiling.

"I've got plenty of pictures of her — really. I half think I left this one out for you, for when you returned." She smiled.

Lela reached out slowly, and allowed herself to take it.

...23

Jim headed out to his car, jacket hitched over his shoulder. This time of year the classrooms could get sticky, if you got enough days without a real breeze. He reveled in the feel of the cool air on his face and looked forward to driving with the windows down.

He turned down his aisle and saw that someone had tucked a flyer under every windshield wiper. That was odd — all the local businesses knew that was prohibited in school parking lots. Had to be some crackpot with a get-rich-quick scheme, or maybe the school was going to repave the lot and needed them all to park somewhere else for a while. He yanked the page free and read it.

FIGHT THE HOMOSEXUAL AGENDA IN YOUR SCHOOL! LESBIAN AND GAY TEACHERS AT FRANKLIN HIGH ARE ENCOURAGING YOUR CHILDREN TO COME OUT OF THE CLOSET. LET YOUR SCHOOL BOARD KNOW THIS IS AN OUTRAGE AND OFFENDERS MUST BE EXPELLED WITHOUT HESITATION! NO, THIS IS NOT JUST THEORY . . . THIS HAS HAPPENED ALREADY AT FRANKLIN HIGH. ASK YOUR SCHOOL BOARD WHY THERE WAS NOT A PUBLIC HEARING ABOUT THIS ISSUE OF GRAVE CONCERN TO PARENTS!

Jim ducked into the car, embarrassed even to be reading such trash. He was sure the flyers were, right now, on cars in the supermarket parking lot and would be in the church lot on Sunday. He knew because that's how it went last year, when Jamie Walsh was first running for the school board, backed by the Christian right groups, percolating with ideas and strong feelings and going on about protecting traditional family values with Policy 6540. The school board had been fairly stodgy before she came along. Her enthusiasm alone seemed to get the attention of parents. To the teachers, she had seemed a comic figure in the beginning, with her fervor about ferreting out some phantom homosexual threat. In the teachers' lounge they had all joked about how they hadn't realized before that there was an epidemic of Franklin High kids going gay. But now that it affected Carly and Donna, it didn't seem so funny.

Besides — he allowed himself a selfish moment — it affected him, didn't it? After all, he was a divorced man, a man who was secretly sleeping with a married woman on the PTO and pleading with her to leave her husband. He knew he wasn't going to win any awards from the religious right, either. But everything with them was about being caught.

Being caught or being sorry. Everybody read in the papers about the Christian ministers who got nabbed for ripping off their churches or keeping secret mistresses across town. Somehow they operated just fine till the woman blew the whistle. And he himself knew at least one rabid right-winger who preached about the sanctity of marriage even while he was divorced himself. Somehow he had managed to put a spin on it so that his followers came to think of his divorce as some naturally occurring freak of nature, like an ice storm in spring, couldn't be held accountable for. As long as you could avoid being found out or, if found out, if you were really, really sorry, you could then flout all the rules. That's what he hated about them.

He turned the car on, opened all the windows and put his head back. Is this what Donna had gotten herself mixed up with? And if she was willing to go this far to keep her idea of her perfect family intact — to herself, to her community — was there any real chance that she'd change her life to be with him?

...24

Lela remembered the diner perfectly well, enough to be able to tell Ann Ellery to meet her in the big red booth in the back by the windows. She and Natalie had always sat here. They'd even tried a cigarette there together for the first time, falling forward on the table in coughing and laughing fits till the waitress had come over to scold them.

When Lela called the paper, she refused to tell Ann Ellery who she was, only that she wanted to talk, off the record, about the Natalie Sheehan suicide ten years ago. The reporter had sounded stern, older than Lela thought she'd be, but obviously curious.

Lela arrived early, wanting to give herself time to confront the ghosts of Natalie in yet another setting. Her head was still swimming from the experience of having been at Natalie's house yesterday, talking with her mother, and she'd hardly slept last night in her motel room from the clamor of all her thoughts and impressions. She knew Kit would have been happy, desperate even, to get a call from her, but she couldn't bring herself to talk to anyone. It felt as if this were just between her and Natalie.

A substitute teacher was covering her classes during the week-long leave of absence she had taken, and Lela wondered what Carly and Fran had heard about the hearing. But her life felt far away, a movie playing on another screen that didn't have much to do with her. Instead, Natalie's life was pressing down on her from all directions. It didn't seem possible that she wouldn't, at any moment, turn a corner and head smiling toward the booth.

Lela spotted Ann Ellery as soon as she pushed through the diner door. She wore black jeans, and a black vest fell loosely over a white short-sleeved T-shirt. Her hair, mostly gray, was combed back behind her ears; that and her narrow face and deep-set eyes gave her a fox-like appearance. She was probably close to fifty, but she walked with a spring that belied her years.

"I'm Ann Ellery," the woman said with the confident voice of someone who was used to her name opening doors or stopping conversation. "With the *Jersey Journal*."

"Yes, I know. You're at the right booth. Thanks for coming." Lela was sure now that Ann Ellery was a lesbian, but she couldn't tell whether the reporter had any suspicions about her.

"Can I know to whom I'm talking, even though this is off the record?" Ann asked, propping a battered black briefcase on the seat next to her.

"I get to ask the questions first, if that's all right," Lela said, smiling faintly.

Ann smiled back. "Fair enough, if I can get some coffee

145

first," she said, gesturing to the waitress. She swallowed down nearly half the cup as soon as it was poured. "Ahhh, hits the spot. I was filing my column pretty late last night."

"How do you pick your topics?" Lela asked, feeling her earlobes begin to burn with anger. "Do you seize on people whose lives it would amuse you to wreck?"

The older woman put her coffee cup down and glared. "Let me explain something. I don't get to have an opinion that doesn't get my name and mug shot on it. If you've got something to say to me, I'd like to know who the hell you are and what it is."

Ann Ellery was more than Lela bargained for; they sized each other up across the gold-flecked diner table. Lela fought hard against the urge to flee the booth, but she told herself that she had to see her mission through. "I'm . . . a friend of Natalie Sheehan's mother. I want to know what it was that you had wanted to write about her daughter all those years ago."

Ann was all squint-eyed scrutiny. Lela could see her weighing the statement for possibilities. "I think you already know."

Lela didn't let herself miss a beat. "What I want to know is why you felt you had a right to write about it."

Ann leaned back against the seat and stared out the window into the parking lot. "Why? I've got a lot of answers." She turned back to Lela. "One, it was a good story. An unfinished story, better yet. Don't look at me like that. I'm a reporter, not a missionary. But that wasn't all, because there are a hundred unfinished stories in a day. I wanted that one because I thought I knew something about it. A great kid died that day, and a second nearly did. I know a few things about teenagers, and one is that if they feel it's worth dying for, it's usually got to do with love. I see two girls on the tracks looking to die, and everybody shifty-eyed and tight-lipped about it, and I put that alongside of the fact that gay kids kill themselves more than other kids, and I figure it's about more than just not being able to find the right dress for the prom."

Lela swallowed hard and tried not to look found out.

"As far as I was concerned," Ann went on, "my paper was part of the conspiracy of silence, because all we did was run two lousy little who-what-where-when stories about it, as if it were just a tree falling over in a lightening storm, as if a thing like that didn't happen because of reasons we could fix, as if it didn't point up a million things that mattered about bigotry and fear and freedom — Jesus, am I making you *cry*?"

"No, I mean, yes, but I'm okay," Lela said, wiping her eyes roughly with a napkin. Her face was hot with humiliation. "Her parents felt you only wanted to blame them."

"I knew that. I tried to explain that they'd go on feeling that way unless they got out from under that silence. Don't you think if those girls had ever seen the word *lesbian* in the paper or in a book or heard it on the radio, without it only ever being attached to losing custody of their kids or being shot in the woods or getting kicked out of their jobs, that maybe they wouldn't have felt like their best option was to check out permanently? Or at least if somebody somewhere had said out loud that it's wrong to do those things to gay people? I'm not saying that there wasn't a soul in Natalie Sheehan's school or town who wouldn't have helped or been sympathetic, but when no one was free to say it, she didn't even have the benefit of knowing there was a dissenting opinion."

"Why didn't you just say that in your column, then? You wouldn't have needed an interview with her parents."

"Well, for one thing, I didn't have the column then. I was just a grunt reporter, so I had to have something newsy to actually report. For two, you can't go around printing that someone is a lesbian without proof, especially if she's just a kid, and you can't always go around saying it even if there *is* proof, unless you can show there's some burning public issue at stake. The way I saw it, there was, but my managing editor finally told me to back the hell off. The parents wrote to him and said I was harassing them. He wanted to know why I was looking to defile the girl's memory anyway. And I said that was exactly why — so someday people would feel being gay wasn't something that defiled you."

Lela sat still and stared at her hands. What Ann was saying was the closest anyone had ever come to saying out loud what had been muzzled inside her own head and heart. The fact that Ann said it without a glance over her shoulder, said it as though she had been saying it all her life, as if it was the truest, most self-evident thing in the universe, was almost too much to absorb.

"What's your connection to Natalie Sheehen's mother?" Ann asked. "Will you tell me that?"

At that moment, Lela made a decision to trust this woman. She was short on allies, and she needed to start somewhere. "I'm Lela Johns," she said quietly.

Ann Ellery stared for a long moment, as if she were trying to memorize her face should she somehow vaporize in front of her. Then she smiled slowly. "It's incredibly wonderful to meet you," she said.

Lela bowed her head; she felt exposed and defenseless. But here, with Ann, she felt also the first glimmer of possibility that maybe what everyone had tried to tell her — that she'd had a right to survive — was true.

"There are about a million things I'd like to ask you," Ann said.

"What I need is for someone else to tell me how this happened to me, some version besides the one I've been telling myself for ten years."

"You mean, some version that doesn't get around to, 'If only I'd done X, she'd be alive today?'"

"Can I get you ladies something else besides coffee?" the waitress, her silver earrings swinging, came over to ask.

"No, a check'll be fine," Ann said. She turned back to Lela. "Look, my apartment's just five minutes from here. Let's go talk there." Lela hesitated. "I'm sorry about the way sounds — I'm not trying to treat you like a cheap date."

Lela laughed, realizing she'd just answered at least one of Ann's unspoken questions. The nuance probably would have been lost on a straight woman.

Lela followed Ann's black Nissan the short distance to her Tudor-style apartment complex. Ann's apartment was on the ground level, and a purring gray cat, his back arched and tail flicking, greeted them as Ann opened the door. "Hey, Pluto," Ann said, shooing him back from the threshold with her foot. "Hope you don't mind cats," she said. "Can I get you something to drink — some juice, maybe?"

"Okay," Lela said, looking around at the apartment, which was really just one big room, the kitchen set off from the living room by only a cooking island, and a writing desk with a computer set up by the television. Lela claimed the leather recliner.

Ann came back in with two glasses of orange juice and a portfolio under her arm. "My clips," she said, opening the binder up and flipping through the pages. "Here," she said, holding it open for Lela, "I don't know if you ever saw this."

HIGH SCHOOL GIRL DIES IN SUSPECTED SUICIDE ON TRAIN TRACKS
by Ann Ellery

OAKWOOD, N.J., April 23, 1986 — A 16-year-old high school junior from St. Ignatius of Antioch High School was killed instantly by a New Jersey Transit train yesterday afternoon in what police are calling a suspected suicide. A second girl, a classmate, was on the tracks with her but fled to safety before the train struck, police reported.

The deceased girl was identified as Natalie Sheehan, a star of the school's basketball team. The identity of the second girl, also 16, who was uninjured, was not released by police, at the request of the school and the parents.

The two girls, both juniors, had apparently lain down across the tracks just as the train was approaching. The train's engineer said he spotted two indistinguishable shapes on the tracks just as his train was coming out of a curve. He tried to brake, but there was insufficient time to stop. He saw one figure jump up at the last moment and flee. A New Jersey Transit spokesman confirmed that the train would have needed at least a half-mile to stop and that visibility out of the curve, where there is no station stop, was less than a quarter of a mile.

A family friend who answered the door at the Sheehan's house in Oakwood said the parents were too devastated to comment.

Students and teachers alike were shocked and grief-stricken when the news reached their school. St. Ignatius is a private, all-girl Catholic institution known for academic excellence. Sister Helena Regis McGowan, the school's principal, made the announcement over the school's public address system shortly after being notified by police. The nun asked the entire student body to pray for both girls and their families, and then dismissed classes for the day.

"We are asking God to help us understand His will at this moment of great sadness," said Sister McGowan when called for comment. She indicated that "wounds would heal faster" if further attention was not called to the death.

"Everybody loved Natalie," said Amy Fitzgibbons, a basketball team mate. "She was really the team's leader, very fun-loving, always joking around. I just can't believe it at all." When asked if Sheehan had seemed depressed of late, Fitzgibbons answered: "Not that I noticed."

A parent, who asked not to be identified, and who showed up at the school to pick up her daughter, said, "Your heart just breaks for the parents. It's so frightening, because you think you know what your kids are thinking and feeling. I know there's going to be a lot of soul-searching going on."

No one questioned at the school was able to characterize the friendship between Sheehan and the unnamed girl, the identity of whom most students seemed to know despite its not being officially released. "I'd see them sometimes in the hall together, and I know they sat together in bio class," said Mary Palatto, a classmate. "But that's about all I know."

"[She's] a serious person, and serious about grades," said Lillian Gault, one of a group of students gathered on a nearby corner, consoling each other. "Some people were kind of surprised that she was hanging out with Natalie, just because Natalie was like the class clown and a jock. But I think they were pretty tight. I don't think they had a lot of other friends besides each other." The unnamed girl is not a member of the basketball team; she is a member of the student book club.

While St. Ignatius has two counselors for its 657 students, the counselors are nuns, without specific psychological training. Students reported that the nuns were mainly religious and academic advisors.

Neal Whorton, an adolescent psychology expert from Rutgers University, warned that teen suicides can come in waves, as teenagers, drawn to the drama such events generate, commit "copycat" suicides.

"Suicide is one of the biggest killers of teenagers and young people," said Whorton. "And yet it's also one of the most preventable. I would strongly urge the administration of St. Ignatius to do widespread, immediate and intense counseling to help students come to grips with their grief, and also to air any confusing feelings they themselves may be having."

It is unclear whether such programs will be put in place at the high school.

The funeral is expected to be held at St. Ignatius of Antioch Church on Thursday morning.

Lela put the book down, her arms quivering as if she had been holding something extremely heavy. It was a strange sensation to see the most intimate event of her life described in such a public and impassive way.

151

"I hope I didn't upset you, showing you this," Ann said. "I really wanted to get around to answering your question about why I wanted to write about Natalie Sheehan." She leaned into the couch. "I mean, this says so little, doesn't it? Just the facts, ma'am. But there was more. When the story broke, my lover at the time was going through a custody battle."

Lela started a little; she was not accustomed to people so casually stating the fact of their sexual preference, certainly not to virtual strangers. Ann Ellery clearly inhabited a whole different world.

"She and I had been together about two years, and she'd been divorced about five years. Her boys were then seven and ten. Her ex-husband had recently gotten remarried and had decided he wanted custody — even though he'd hardly bothered to see the boys before then, let alone paid a cent in support." She put her head back and sighed. "See, Maggie had met him when she was working as a parole officer. He'd done time for manslaughter. Seems he'd gotten drunk and shoved his girlfriend around and she'd lost her footing and fallen down a flight of stairs and broken her neck. He convinced Maggie it was an accident and he was a changed man, and she fell in love. They got married and had these two kids — except then he started shoving her around, too." Ann sighed and shook her head. "Anyway, when he sued her for custody, his claim was that his boys were turning into fairies, and the fact that they lived with two dykes was the reason. He said the boys showed no interest in sports, they were overly fussy about their clothes — I know, I know, incredibly dumb and offensive stuff. And of course Maggie's lawyer brought up the obvious — that he'd been absent, abusive, and there was this little matter of his having killed his girlfriend."

Lela felt her heart pounding as Ann was talking, hoping she was wrong about how the story would turn out.

"But the judge — a man — said he believed the girlfriend incident had been an accident. Not admirable behavior, granted, but an accident that the guy shouldn't be punished for forever, and that it really was more harmful for the boys to be living in a lesbian household, especially when they had this wholesome option of living with their loving father and his new wife."

"Tell me you're making this up," Lela said, gingerly stroking Pluto, who'd curled up in her lap.

"I wish I were. Maggie was just leveled. She didn't have any money left for an appeal, and no lawyer wanted to take it pro bono. Too long a shot. You can guess it didn't do a lot for our relationship. Every time she looked at me, she had to face the fact that she'd lost her boys because of me —"

"It *wasn't* because of you."

"Well, no, of course not. Not when you kept the big picture in view. But at the end of the day, what it came down to was that I got into bed beside her, and the boys were not in their rooms down the hall anymore. All that hatred toward the judge and the system and the ex — it had to seep out some- where. I had offered to leave earlier. I told her she could tell the judge she was done with me, done with women — what- ever — but she didn't want to hear it. She needed me to get through it. I was the only friend in the world she had. Besides, neither one of us really thought she'd lose custody to a murderer! Plus, we also thought we'd have on our side the fact that the boys were happy and healthy, and they'd only ever lived with their mom. So when it really happened, when she really lost them, it was like slamming into a brick wall at about a hundred miles an hour. You don't get put back together again the same way. Every day it got worse, that feeling that I had cost her the boys. So I left."

Lela turned the story over and over in her mind, recoiling at its horrors. "I'm so sorry," she whispered.

"Yeah," Ann said, sitting up. "So Natalie's story —" she looked across the room at her — "*your* story — hit me hard. I felt in my gut you were one of our own. And while I couldn't do a thing about my own personal life having been shredded up by hatred and prejudice, by God, I wanted to do something,

153

somewhere. And yeah, I wanted to hold people accountable. I admit it — I was partly angry at the parents. I couldn't get over the idea that they should have been able to see it coming. Maybe they were right to stay away from me. But I was really gunning for more than that. I was after the church and the school and the students and the whole goddamn world. It wasn't personal, especially," she said, laughing.

"How did you go on?"

"Living is the best revenge, sometimes. But that's really what I wanted to ask you."

It was only the second time Lela had ever told the whole story — the first time was to Kit — but this time, telling it to Ann, she suddenly saw some of the details a little differently. This time she felt sorrow for Natalie's sake alone, without the barbed-wire entanglement of guilt. She talked for hours, and Ann never ran out of questions, or sympathy. Before Lela knew it, the sun was slipping down the sky, and Ann had taken off her vest and was preparing a salad and boiling water for pasta, all while Lela kept talking. It wasn't until they were nearly done with the meal that Lela got around to the whole mess with Carly and the school board hearing.

Ann started collecting their plates and carrying them to the sink. "They're looking for a sacrifice, you know that. What are you going to do?"

"I don't feel like I have a lot of options. I can quit now, or I can quit later, after I can't stand any more of the kind of exile they've made for me."

"There's always option three."

"Oh, let me guess — be a martyr," Lela said.

"If you're going to leave anyway, you might as well fight them," Ann said, loading the dishwasher. "If you come out, you'll finally get to confront the real guts of it. Right now all you're doing is arguing silly details on their terms. And meanwhile, they get to hint all over the place that you're some evil lesbian seducer who probably has locker-room pinups of the girls' basketball team in her bedroom —"

"Stop! I don't even want to *hear* this!"

"Lela," Ann said, walking over and seizing her by the shoulders. "You better get used to it. That's G-rated stuff. It could get much worse. And they'll say it anyway, whether you come clean about being a dyke or not. In fact, they're probably counting on your not admitting it, which suits them even better. Because then no one calls them to the mat to explain exactly how it is that you can still be a bigot about this in America."

Lela rubbed her eyes. "Look, the fact is I signed a contract to teach in a school where I knew they had this 6540 policy. Besides, before the week is out, Jamie Walsh is going to have them convinced that I lured the entire junior class to my apartment for lesbian sex lessons."

"But you see, if you keep dodging her, she doesn't have to stick to the facts. You have to walk right up to what they're saying and say what's true and what isn't. That you are a lesbian, but that you're not a threat to their daughters. And that for their daughters who are already lesbians, you are a hedge against the kind of despair that actually costs lives."

"Oh, now you're really fantasizing! So now they're not only going to accept that *I'm* a lesbian, but that their *daughters* are?"

"I know — I'm an optimist. It helps you survive, though, when you're part of a despised minority."

Lela laughed. She was pretty sure it was the first time she'd felt like it in a week, maybe longer. She had come here to catalogue her losses; she never planned to go home richer, to make a friend. "Well, what about you? Are they okay about you're being so out at the paper?"

"Sure, in a way. But I still have to teach them every day. The times I don't want to write about a lesbian or feminist issue, my editor still demands to know how it fits my column. He think it's like a sports columnist who suddenly wants to comment on the new Calvin Klein collection. I have to tell him, Hey, I live in the *whole world*. I don't just glide along on some lesbian parallel universe, where only lesbian things happen to me."

155

Lela smiled, and yet the sadness was ebbing back. "I wish now they had let you write about Natalie. You would have done her story justice."

"Well, her parents weren't ready. It's okay."

"I let her down in so many ways I keep discovering. I should have —"

"Shhhhh, don't." Ann reached out slowly and touched a fingertip to Lela's lips. "You and Natalie Sheehan had different fates. You've got to live out yours."

Lela's stomach crimped in fear. For so long she had felt her life crowded into Natalie's shadow. Going on without her was something she'd avoided for a decade. Did she have the courage to do it now?

Lela headed back into the living room, where Pluto was asleep on top of the TV. Ann followed her. "Is someone expecting you home tonight?" Ann asked. "Because if not, you can crash here. You must be exhausted."

"Oh, no, I couldn't. I'm sure you've had about all you can take of me for a day," Lela said.

Ann came over and joined her on the couch. It was the first time all day Lela thought she seemed hesitant. "The trouble is," Ann said, "when it comes to you, I could just be getting started."

A slow wave of warmth rolled up Lela's neck and into her cheeks. "I can't," Lela said. "You've been . . . I mean, this whole day has been . . ."

"It's okay," Ann said. "I'm out of line. But just promise me you won't disappear again."

Lela regarded her for a moment. "I won't," she said. And she wondered if she could mean it.

...25

It was nearly dinnertime, and Carly was not home from school yet. She should have been home hours ago, and Donna had just begun to get anxious. There was no one she could talk to, either. Hugh was away again and Craig had gone straight from baseball practice to have dinner at a friend's house. Her family's fractured habits were how Donna had been able to have the house so much to herself, for her and Jim, in the first place.

She thought of him now with longing. There was a new tension between them over the school board battle. She hadn't expected that. She had expected him to fully support her, to be a balm over the pain Carly had caused. That he disagreed with her, more strongly each time they talked about it, scared her, because she saw no way to resolve it — even as she was facing the fact that she was not prepared to lose him.

But more than anything, she worried about Carly. If her daughter had any real idea what it meant to be a lesbian, she would not be saying she was one, Donna was sure of that. In front of the school board, she'd argued that Carly had been completely corrupted, but privately she did not — could not — believe that. She was a bright, sensitive girl, and boys this age could be crude and klutzy. Factor in some glamorous-seeming teacher espousing lesbian theories, and even a girl like Carly might decide it was a smarter, more sophisticated lifestyle. But Donna would not let her go a step farther down that treacherous path. Except that every time she tried to talk to Carly about boys or Lela Johns or Fran Reilly, they had terrible fights. The school board action prompted a fresh wave of rage — Carly had gone something close to crazy, screaming and crying, saying over and over how unfair it was, how bigoted, how stupid, how wrong. Donna had desperately tried to get a foothold, to explain how Lela Johns had used bad judgment, how she had overstepped, how she had abused her authority. But Carly had only defended her more fiercely and with more emotion as their shouting got louder.

Donna stood in the middle of the kitchen, staring out the window into the backyard. Even though they'd sold the swing set years ago, she still pictured it out there, with Carly on it, soaring back and forth, her toes aimed at the sky. The start of spring always used to excite her so because it meant she could get back on her swing set, and Donna had loved it, too, being able to watch her little girl outside while she inside making dinner. But tonight she would not cook. She wasn't up to it. Besides, it would just be the two of them, and these days Carly always preferred pizza or take-out chicken, anyway.

"I hate living here! You're ruining my life! I can't stand it anymore!" Carly had screamed at her last night, and it was the single most terrifying of all the things she'd hurled at her.

Because in the most basic way, Carly *was* out of her control. She walked out of the house in the morning and negotiated the world on her own. It shocked Donna every time she thought of it, knowing how unconscious kids could be and how many ways they could put themselves in harm's way. Donna still had to fight the urge to reach for Carly's hand when they were crossing the street together, and yet, in a year, Carly would be able to drive a car by herself. It boggled Donna's mind. So if Carly were crazy enough to run away, to get into strangers' cars and have them drop her off in the middle of nowhere, Donna knew she wouldn't be able to physically stop her. And that was maddening.

She went to the front window, peeked through the parted curtains. If Carly wasn't home by seven, Donna was going to call the police, that was all there was to it. She had never been this late before.

So when the phone rang, her heart leapt.

"Hi, Donna," Cathy Reilly said. "Look, I was just wondering . . . Franny isn't home yet and that's not like her. It's her night to baby-sit her little sisters while I go to my bowling league, and I haven't even had as much as a phone call from her saying she'll be late."

Donna felt her scalp tingle with fear. Could Carly have run off with this nitwit girl Fran? Should she get in the car and go out looking for them herself? But where would she look? Then a new thought filled her with rage: she knew they should have demanded to know where Lela Johns had gone during her week of leave. She might have arranged to have the girls meet her. "Oh, my God," Donna said.

"What?" Cathy Reilly said. "Do you know where she is?"

"No, but we'll find her," Donna said. "We'll find them all."

...26

Lela circled the spot several times, afraid to do what she'd come to do. Her upper lip remained clammy, no matter how many times she wiped it.

She parked, finally, and sat with the window cracked and the radio low. She thought about the commuters away at jobs, people for whom the railroad tracks were purely functional, a logistical fact of life. For her, they were a macabre shrine, a place of death, not just Natalie's, but in a way her own.

She got out and squinted into the sun. April twenty-second, ten years to the day. She looked down the shallow hill, the one she'd once stumbled down, screaming, struggling to understand how Natalie had gone from being her lover to being their executioner. She started slowly down the hill — it was not nearly as steep or long as it had grown in her memory — and stopped well before the tracks. She couldn't imagine going any closer; she was trembling even at this distance of fifty feet or so.

She crouched, pulling up clumps of grass, yanking a whole patch bald, suddenly sobbing into her knees. She was here to ask what she had never been able to ask Natalie for before, not that day, not since: to let her go. "I didn't *want* to go with you! I wanted to live!" she yelled into the ground, her ribs aching with her sobs. This was the very thing that had saved her, and yet it was also her failure. Because she had said, *Only this far, and no further,* and that made her unworthy of Natalie, and unworthy in her own eyes, forever.

She would always believe it, but now she wanted to at least stop living it. She wanted to be pardoned, wanted to live the life she had gotten by giving Natalie up. That was the thing none of them had understood: how her survival was its own tragedy because Natalie had slipped through some audacious assumption, found some invisible trap door that said you didn't have to go on living, if living was all pain. It was a relief, for some, to find that door, to push hard enough on it and find it giving way. But it had snapped shut behind Natalie that day, and there had not been room enough for two. No one had known how Lela had felt — like a coward, a charlatan — running up this hill alone, escaping one despair for another, the train screeching through behind her on exactly the mission Natalie had assigned it.

Lela rocked backward and sat down, hugging her knees to her chin. She had wanted to come here this time not in terror, but on her own terms. She wanted some kind of sign that Natalie was here, or that she was once here, or if not here, then somewhere else entirely so that she didn't need

Lela anymore. But the hill and tracks were unmoving. Nothing stirred, neither blackbirds nor squirrels, not an oncoming train. Just like last time, there was no one to help her.

Out of her jacket pocket, Lela took Natalie's picture, the one Mrs. Sheehan had given her, in its simple gold frame, and began to dig with a rock. She wedged the picture into its small grave, studied the image one last time, and then pushed the earth over it, patting it down with her open palm. She hurt from some untraceable source; her breath in her throat was like fire. She wanted Natalie to stay put now. She wanted to go on without her.

...27

Dear Ms. Johns:

I feel terrible about everything's that happened, and I feel like that's all I've been saying to you since I've known you. You're probably sorry I ever crossed your path. I don't know how I'm ever going to make it up to you for all the trouble I've caused you. When my mother told me about the school board having that Inquisition thing — and how proud she was for being the ring leader — I just screamed and screamed. I've never felt so far away from my mom — I don't even recognize her. I guess she feels *the same way about me, now that she knows I'm queer. I think we used to be close — she has all these pictures around of her and me as a baby, and she really looks, you know, enraptured, like they say in romance novels, when she looks at them. I guess she thinks she's doing the right thing — you know, protecting me from lesbian influences!!!! — but she's so out of touch that I can't stand to be near her right now. I'm praying you're not being held responsible for my running off, too, but if I am — oh God, here I go again — I'm so, so sorry.*

I'm in California, as you can see from the envelope, and I'm with Fran, as you maybe guessed. We're not a perfect couple, I guess you guessed that, too. But there are a lot of things about her that I love, and we're getting to spend so much time together alone, and that's been <u>incredible</u>. And really, Fran is the reason we're not homeless and starving. One of her older friends has friends out here, and they've let us stay with them. They're about an hour outside of San Francisco. We're kinda like local heroes. They call us Lesbians on the Loose, Lesbians at Large, that kind of thing.

I just wanted you to know I'm all right. I haven't written to anyone else. I hope my sending you this letter doesn't get you into <u>more</u> trouble. You should probably throw this out once you get it. Not that it would help anyone find us — you see there's no return address. I don't know how long we'll be away. Fran won't even talk about going back. But I'll write to you again.

I guess I also wanted to say how cool I think you are. I mean, you've done a lot for me — even if you don't know it.

Love,
Carly

It was the first piece of mail Lela opened when she got back to her apartment. *Ran away, they ran away.* Lela could have told her that wouldn't solve anything. But Carly was right about one thing: The school probably would find some way to blame her for this, too.

There was other mail, too: a letter from the school board, confirming that she had been given a warning — as though she could have somehow forgotten. And a "missing you" card from Kit.

She got up and went to the phone. Kit. She had so much to tell her.

Kit was at her front door in less than a half-hour, and while Lela was glad to see her, she dodged the kiss Kit aimed at her lips. She glossed over the awkward moment by quickly handing her Carly's letter to read.

"I wouldn't be surprised," Kit said, visibly worried, "if they think there's some kind of lesbian Underground Railroad and you put them on it. Oh, Jesus — railroad, I'm sorry . . . I didn't think."

"It's okay," Lela said. "I'm the one who has to learn to stop seeing everything through the prism of 'what happened to me and Natalie.' And I'm going to." Lela could see that Kit didn't trust that some strange outburst was not far behind. "Did anything else happen while I was away?"

"Yes, as a matter of fact," Kit said, following Lela into the kitchen. "Everyone in town got these horrible flyers in the mail saying there's a homosexual conspiracy at Franklin, teachers who are encouraging your kids to come out of the closet. Sent anonymously, of course. When word gets out that Carly and Fran high-tailed it to the gay capitol of the Western Hemisphere, it's going to look like these doomsayers are right. I guess Donna Matson and Jamie Walsh have the paper cuts to show for all their work."

"Oh, they get help from the national groups, too, don't kid yourself," Lela said. Ann had given her a crash course in the mechanisms of hate politics. "The big groups monitor this kind of local skirmish, hoping they can do a lot of damage while they fly underneath the radar of national media coverage. This way the parents have no real counterpoint to the hysterics they stir up."

"Are you — I mean, did you change your mind about going back to school?" They settled onto the couches in the living room. Kit popped open a beer and tucked her legs underneath her.

"No. In fact, I'm more determined to go back than ever. The school board's not going to tell me how to live my life."

Kit smiled. "I don't think this is the effect they thought the probation would have."

"It's not the probation," Lela said. She quickly told Kit the whole story of the week and how moved she had been by Mrs. Sheehan's and Ann Ellery's stories.

"Well, even so, you're going to have to be on your best behavior in class."

"Oh, right — no more wearing those 'No One Knows I'm Queer' T-shirts to school," Lela said, shaking her head. "I was *always* one of the most conservative people there."

"Well, now you have to be one of the most conservative people on the planet. So, like, I don't know . . . don't call on any of the girls, for example."

"I won't teach like that!" Lela said, frowning. "What are you smiling at?"

"You. You sounded like a teacher just then. Like you care how you do it. I haven't heard you talk like that before."

"I know, but —"

"Don't apologize, for God's sake! It's great."

Lela crushed a throw pillow against her. "I realized — I think in Mrs. Sheehan's dining room — that if a single adult person had ever said to Natalie or me that we weren't crazy for feeling what we felt . . ."

"Don't do that to yourself," Kit said.

166

"No, it's okay. I mean, I'm beginning to accept that nothing I could have said would have stopped Natalie. We needed some adult gay person to say, 'I did it. I grew up. I'm happy. You can be, too.' God, ten years ago was all it was. But it was the dark ages. Carly's already got a hundred times the options we had."

"Well," Kit said, "it's still not a cake walk for her. This isn't Yale or anything. When you're sixteen in the suburbs, they're still pushing proms and weddings down your throat. And her very own school board is still trying to nail you to the proverbial pink triangle."

"I just wish we could get the girls to come home," Lela said. "Maybe we can get the word out to everyone we know in San Francisco and Guerneville."

"And say what? Question every sixteen-year-old girl you see on the street? Send home by Fed Ex?"

"Something not far off that." She got up and headed for the kitchen wall phone. "Come on, we can start calling now — it's still early on the West Coast."

"Feeling optimistic these days?" Kit said, getting up.

"I hear," Lela said, "that it takes practice."

...28

As Lela passed through Franklin's front door and made her way down the corridor, it took her a beat to recognize the feeling: intense self-consciousness, shame, fear. It was how she'd felt at sixteen, when she'd gone back to St. Ignatius after Natalie was dead. She'd had to retrieve stuff from her locker and sign some papers with her mother about the transfer, and she'd felt the hallways alive with judgmental eyes. She wondered now if some of the kids had actually been welcoming, or admiring, or sympathetic, but at the time she was convinced they were all damning and mocking her.

She told herself now that probably far fewer of the kids

168

than she imagined had heard about her probation — let alone the details — and even fewer than that were likely to care. Or so Kit had tried to convince her in the pep talk she had delivered before she'd left last night.

Lela turned the corner, past the doors to the gym, past the wall of olive green lockers, toward the teacher's lounge. It was a beautiful spring morning, and it seemed to want to burst through the windows into the tile hallways. The kids would be feeling it, too; their blood would be moving a little quicker. She remembered what it felt like to have the summer and all its unscheduled pleasures just within reach. As a teacher, your classes in the spring had to be that much more interesting. She felt just edgy enough today to be up to the challenge.

When she pushed open the doors to the lounge, a hush fell over the room. A cluster of her colleagues by the coffee machine attempted stiff-shouldered nonchalance; another group turned back to their conversations with forced smiles. She felt dabs of sweat at her hairline, the beginning of a pant high in her throat. She'd never had an attack at school, and she didn't plan to start now. So she scooped her mail out of her box — and there was a lot of it — bundled it under her arm and headed for her office.

As she neared the office, she saw that the door was already open. That gave her time to set her face. "Hey, Jim," she said when she went in, not meeting his eyes.

"Oh, welcome back," he said, clearly startled.

She wheeled her chair close to her desk and started sorting her mail, hoping Jim would not try for small talk. A lot of what she'd gotten was junk notices, but she quickly zeroed in on a package of pink carbon forms, all paper-clipped together. "Notice of Student Dropping Class," read the top of each sheet. She scanned the pile. Twelve girls had dropped her morning English class, the one that started in twenty minutes. That left only eleven kids, just three of those girls. Six kids — also all girls — had dropped the afternoon session, and ten more were out of her Tuesday-Thursday class.

169

She sucked in her breath; to drop out this late in the semester was unheard of. And the other English teachers had to be severely overloaded with her students because of it. That was sure not to win her any support.

She scanned the forms again; at the bottom, there was a section for "Reason Dropping Class." Checked off for each and every girl was "parental request." Her heart was a fist against her ribs.

"Lela," Jim said, his voice seeming to come from a long way off. "I just want you to know I think it's sickening what they're doing to you."

She whirled around. What reason at all did she have to trust him? For all she knew he was pledged to spy on her and gather more ammunition for the school board. And then there was a new thought: if he was sincerely outraged on her behalf, it was only because he would think that being accused of lesbianism was an ugly thing, and clearly not possible in the case of a woman he considered pretty enough to want to date.

He looked away and tugged at his beard. "Look, it's okay, you don't have to talk about it. I just want you to know that I believe the policy and the tactics are a threat to all teachers. I'm a divorced man — should I have a chaperone, too, anytime I want to counsel a girl on Chaucer in my office? Jesus, statistics show they've got more reason to worry about me than you." He shook his head, pointlessly straightened some papers on his desk. "I, uh, tried to tell some of our esteemed colleagues this, but, ah, most of them are a bunch of sheep. They think this has got nothing to do with them, and won't ever, and they just want to steer clear of you like the plague."

Lela realized she was gripping the arms of her chair as though she were on a plane bound for a rough landing. This was a side of Jim she didn't know. But then, she really didn't know any side of him, did she? She had been so busy walling herself off, staring down the dark corridors of her own psyche, that she hadn't really seen anyone around her. Could he be genuine? "How do you know about the chaperone part?" she asked.

"How?" He laughed. "The school board is the least discreet body of quasi-professionals there is. Besides, they seem especially interested in getting the word out about this. You must know Jamie Walsh's history and ambition level?"

"I've been filled in," Lela said.

"Okay, and now that the girls have run off, she's especially puffed up with righteous indignation. For her own sake, of course. I've never seen her say or do a single thing solely to ease parents' suffering."

Now it was Lela's turn to look down. She was desperate not to betray any inkling that she knew of Carly and Fran's whereabouts — or else there would be no making anyone believe she hadn't been in on it from the beginning. "That's the worst part of this whole thing, the toll it must be taking on the girls."

"Kids have run off before at Franklin. It's always handled privately, the less said the better. This is the first time I've seen it broadcast from the rooftops, and treated as a conspiracy."

"Is that what they're saying? People think I had something to do with the girls' running away?"

"One way or the other, they do. Either that the girls are afraid of you, or confused or, yeah, that you helped them leave their mothers' bosoms. The parents were practically told they were leaving their daughters in your classes at their own risk. And even if they didn't feel their own daughters were at personal risk, it was important to send a message that you weren't to be supported."

Lela picked up the stack of "drops" again. Who were all these parents, so ready to believe the worst of her? "How long do you think I've got, Jim?"

He shook his head. "I don't know, Lela. But I suggest you make the most of it."

171

29

Hugh had come home the first night Donna had called, jumping on the last flight out of Chicago. It wasn't an easy meeting to leave — he'd had a presentation to give the next afternoon — so he was feeling pretty deserving of some credit by the time he got home. Instead, Donna had barely looked up when he'd come in, just continued to sit on the couch and stare the way he suspected she'd been doing since she first realized Carly was missing.

This was their eighth day of the vigil, as Hugh had come to think of it, sitting huddled in the living room, sometimes with Craig, sometimes not, as if Carly would just show up, having lost track of her curfew by a week and a day. The local and state police had been called; the FBI was officially notified. Carly and this girl Fran — whoever she was, he had never once laid eyes on her — were classified as runaways, because there had been fights and threats of all kinds right before the disappearance. Hugh was stunned that Donna hadn't thought to lie — to say that the kid had spent the week sewing slippers for the whole family to the tune of Christian music so the lazy s.o.b.s in law enforcement would do their jobs. It was only if they suspected foul play that they would move their butts. What did Donna expect them to say when she told them she and the kid had been at each other's throats all week? What did *he* expect, she screamed back, given that he was hardly ever there when his family needed him. But most of the time, nobody made him feel needed till after the fact, when he could be blamed for something.

All this meant that Carly's disappearance into thin air didn't make the news, the way it did when the authorities thought someone had taken your little girl and sold her into the sex trade or ground her up into mulch. There wasn't much else he and Donna could do, except sit and think. He was sure of one thing: Carly would come back. All she wanted was to give her mother a wake-up call, let her know that she wasn't a kid anymore, that she was going to make her own decisions, whatever those decisions were. Hugh didn't pretend to know. He was just relieved she hadn't run off with a guy, come home knocked up, something like that. Not that two girls alone on the road couldn't end up getting into plenty of trouble with guys, but it seemed like her plan was to stick to packs of women, and this was one scenario where he was grateful for that.

He and Donna hadn't had this much uninterrupted time together since their honeymoon, and he realized that all his work trips had helped forestall the inevitable. They were dead to each other, unable to console each other in their pain, unwilling to embrace the other's ideas, uninterested in the other's future. He'd long felt proprietary about her — he liked to say "my wife" — but these days it didn't feel any more intimate to him than saying "my accountant" or "my contractor." She had to feel it, too, and then some, probably. He suspected she hated him — real, honest-to-God hatred. What he couldn't figure out was how they'd come this far without her saying she wanted him to go.

They sat in the living room, he in his favorite chair, she on the couch, as had become their ritual.

"This is the cruelest thing she could have done to me — pure, inexcusable torture. I didn't know she was capable of such cruelty," Donna announced. She recited a version of this every hour, sometimes elaborating, sometimes not. She hadn't eaten at all. He had succeeded in getting her to have some broth, something like every other day. That he was able to eat normal meals disgusted her.

"Donna, she doesn't mean it to hurt you. She's only thinking of herself, how much fun she's having."

She looked at him with what he took to be unbridled revulsion. "Of *course* she means it to hurt me. She means it to rip my heart out. That's what the fun of it *is*. But how would you expect to know a thing about her? You're hardly ever here, and when you are you make no effort with the kids at all, not one bit."

They'd had this argument a hundred different times since the night he'd come home. He was just playing his part now — it hardly meant a thing to him, her insults. But she seemed to mean it afresh every time, even when her words hardly varied.

"Besides, everyone is so goddamn sure she is having a good time," she continued. "It's infuriating! No one knows that! These cops. We don't know that she wasn't kidnapped, that whoever else she's with won't let her come home, or even call." Her voice broke, and she looked at the phone. "No one knows for sure that she's safe. No one can tell me that. And I seem to be the only one who cares! The rest of you are acting like it's a perfectly normal thing for Carly to

174

go off for a week. She's sixteen, in case you've lost track. She's just a baby!"

"She's not a baby, Donna. You're going to have to get a different attitude when she comes back, or she's not going to be back for long."

"Don't you threaten me. Suddenly you've got all these ideas about how to raise her? Suddenly you're all interested? No matter how thankful to God I'll be that she is home safe and sound, she is still going to have to answer for what she did. You think that's what you do — let your kids wipe their feet all over you? Do whatever the hell they feel like, from staying out all night to running with a bunch of lesbians, and leaving home?"

"This lesbian stuff, Donna, she'll get over it." The way he figured it, she just hadn't met a man yet who'd made an impression. It was fine by him if she wanted to diddle around with other girls in the meantime — it'd keep her from getting knocked up. And she'd come around to wanting a man before long. All women did, except the really twisted ones, and his daughter wasn't twisted.

"Unbelievable. You're all so brilliant and know Carly so well — why don't any of you know where the hell she is? Why don't you just go out and get her and bring her home?"

This particular line of attack never failed to break his cool. Donna wouldn't believe him if he told her, but if anybody *had* hurt Carly, he'd kill him, no question about it. Even if he had to rot in jail the rest of his life, he'd be a happier man than being free and knowing that whoever did it was alive. He didn't want to think about that, though, so he switched on the television. It was time for the ten o'clock news.

"I'm going up to bed. Don't wake me when you come up," she said.

He tried to stop himself, but the words were out by the time she hit the second step. "Donna, when this is all over, I just thought you should know, I'm leaving you."

She froze on the stairs, the way you did when you forgot

what it was that you were heading for and were searching your mind. The whole house, the very air in it, felt weirdly still. A thin film of sweat broke out over his upper lip. Now that it was out, he did not regret having said it — but he did regret that it was true, that he couldn't make her be more like the woman he first fell in love with, that she wouldn't do a thing to try to change his mind.

After a moment, she continued up the stairs, as if he'd said nothing at all out of the ordinary.

...30

Lela was running late — there had been an accident that tied up traffic — and when she pushed open the door to her class, she found the kids in a heated shouting match.

"Hey, hey, what's going on here?" she yelled. "I'm ten minutes late and I can't count on you guys to remain civilized?" She slammed her canvas bag down on her desk, silencing them. This was Carly's and Fran's class, and Lela had been bracing herself for some kind of confrontation since she'd been back. "Somebody want to tell me what the battle's about? Somehow I doubt it has to do with Sinclair Lewis."

The class was down to eleven kids — half its pre-school-board action size. Lela knew the remaining kids knew why their classmates were missing; what she didn't know was how they felt about it. Maybe today she'd find out. She scanned their faces for clues. She settled on Tim Cox, fidgeting in his seat.

"Tim, you want to get me up to speed here?" He said nothing, but his face turned bright red, the color creeping clear up his forehead, under his strawberry-blond hairline. "I'm perfectly content to keep you all here for as long as it takes, until somebody tells me what's going on."

"That's not what I hear," came a male voice from the back. "I hear you're in more trouble than any of us'll ever be." A spray of titters broke out from his vicinity.

"You don't need to concern yourself with my career, Ron," Lela said, sounding calmer than she felt. Ron Banks, son of Mr. and Mrs. Banks. Put them on the list. Probably figured she wouldn't hurt their son, since she was clearly only into little girls, but she was fair game to trash, anyway. Her legs were trembling; she sat down, afraid it might show. "Is that what you were all arguing over?"

"Sort of," Melissa McGrath said. She was a bright, un-attractive girl, contentious about her homework, but someone who had never been a real presence in the room before now. "We were talking about Carly and Fran. Tell Ms. Johns what you said about them, Tim."

Tim shot Melissa a look that would have stopped your blood in its veins had it come from a stranger on a deserted street. "I was just saying," Tim said defiantly, "that there isn't a lezzie out there that a good screw couldn't fix — even if she fought you off in the beginning."

Ron guffawed his encouragement, but everyone else just shifted quietly.

Don't lose it, Lela told herself. It was nothing. He was showing off, mouthing the kind of mindless obscenity that teenage boys have for centuries. But then again, it was everything. It was exactly the kind of moment that might save someone's life. Maybe one of these other kids was gay, or maybe one of them would be away at college one day with a friend who decided to go gay-bashing for kicks one night. If Lela didn't say right now without reservation what was right and what was wrong, who would, and when?

"Sexual orientation is innate, Tim, and you don't get to go around 'fixing' it any more than you get to go around 'fixing' someone's race," Lela said, her mouth growing more dry with every word. "Not in this country in this century, anyway. Besides, it sounds to me an awful lot that your prescription is rape, and I'd like to remind you that that's a crime — a serious one — so I don't recommend that you practice it *or* preach it."

Melissa started to clap, slowly at first, and then more emphatically as a half dozen of the other kids joined her. Lela felt lightheaded with relief. Tim kept scowling down at his desk, and then abruptly swept his books into his backpack and stomped out. Ron followed him.

"Anyone else?" Lela asked. She had just a handful of kids left — three girls, six boys — but each one meant more to her than the entire class had meant before. They all looked at her expectantly. "Okay then, let's get back to *Main Street*."

"They didn't waste any time, did they?" Kit asked, after Lela read her over the phone the school board notice demanding her presence at a hearing the following night at 7:30.

"Rita told me the night appointment is so that parents can come," Lela said.

"God, it makes me crazy," Kit said, fussing with the pillow at her back. It was late, after eleven; she had been in bed when Lela called. "None of this would be happening if they'd just let the girls live their own lives. If only they could know how happy they are right now."

"Look, Kit, I know I can't stop you from coming tomorrow night but you can't get up and say something like that."

"I know that," Kit said. "But you've got to let me do something for you." She sighed. "I wish the girls were here themselves. I've called everybody I've ever known since grade school who's living anywhere in the Bay area, and we don't have even a sighting."

"The damage is already done, though. Jamie Walsh can still say they ran — and will be back safe only by the grace of God."

"All right then, let me call Mrs. Sheehan and Ann Ellery. Let me tell them to come and say what happens when you leave a couple of teenagers emotionally marooned and do nothing to help!"

"I'm not going to ask anybody else to suffer over this. Mrs. Sheehan has been through hell and back. I'd never ask her to do this, especially not for my sake."

"No one can help you, is that it?" Kit said, angry for the first time on this point. "Because you couldn't save Natalie Sheehan, no one is ever able to put a hand out to you? Why don't you let people take their own risks? She can say no if she wants. She's a grown woman. It might do her some good to help."

"Don't ask them, Kit. Either one of them. And don't do it behind my back. I won't thank you for it, even it made a difference, which it won't."

Kit knew Lela was serious but she was going to do it anyway, she decided, even if it cost her Lela's trust, and more. She loved her too much not to try.

"We should get some sleep," Kit said, promising nothing as they hung up. She switched off the TV and the lamps and lay still in her bed, watching the room take shape in the dark.

...32

Donna had read the letter so many times that she could recite it by heart.

Dear Mom,
I know you're worried and I didn't want you thinking the whole time I was dead on the roadside somewhere. I also didn't want you thinking that anybody else but me made me run away. It was my decision and I wanted to do it. I had to do it. What I wanted you thinking about instead is the fact that maybe I am not the daughter you thought I'd turn

*out to be, but I am who I am and you can fire the
entire staff of Franklin and it won't change a thing.
Fran and I are safe and happy. I don't know exactly
when we'll be home, but it'll be soon.*

Love,
Carly

Donna had already pictured a thousand different settings
for Carly while she was writing it, already read a thousand
different meanings into each sentence. The one immutable
fact was the letter itself, of course. If Carly had thought to
write and send it, then things between them were not
irreparable.

She thought this over again as Jim, sitting in the passenger seat next to her, read the letter himself. She'd allowed
herself to leave the house for a little while since the letter
had arrived; it was one prayer answered, so she thought it
was safe to take a break from their vigil. She'd shown the
letter to police, and while they said it would help them
possibly find her, they were clearly a little less motivated
since it was plain now that Carly was a garden-variety runaway.

"Well, that *is* good news, isn't it, that she's safe," Jim said,
handing back the letter.

"The first I've had in a week and a half," Donna said.
She'd had to see him when the letter came; she couldn't talk
to him from the house, not with Hugh underfoot. She'd
asked him to meet her on South Hendricks Road. It was an
out-of-the-way little street behind the lumber yard that most
people in town found only when they were badly lost. Jim's
car was parked just ahead of them; he was staring straight
ahead at it now. "I've missed you, Jim," she said. "I haven't
been out of the house or talked to anyone since Carly's been
gone."

"Except Hugh," Jim said.

"Well, he's in the house. He came home, he had to —

how would it look otherwise? But we haven't done much but cut into each other." She wished he would look at her, really look at her, the way he did when they were alone. She slid her hand over and rested it on his thigh. Her relief suddenly gave way to a giddy stirring and she half considered suggesting they grope each other like teenagers. "Didn't you miss me?"

He looked at her finally. "I can't do this anymore, Donna." He was out of patience; she could hear it in his voice. She supposed she knew it would come to this.

"What do you mean?" she asked, playing dumb anyway, hoping he might lose his nerve.

"I mean *this* — sneaking around like a criminal. I hate it. There's no good reason for it, either, except hypocrisy, and I refuse to be party to that anymore. This whole thing with the school board has been the last straw — it's made me see things clearly."

Her gut tightened. "What does that have to do with anything?" She pulled her hand back.

"See, that's the problem."

"What are you talking about?"

"You don't seem to give a shit about hearing Carly out — you just want people around her punished."

"Oh, don't be such a simpleton, Jim! Of course I want her to be, to get well-adjusted or whatever —"

"No! No, you don't! You just want her *fixed*. You want it all the way *you* want it to be. You want to be a husband and wife who made the right choice from the time you said 'I do' and never get divorced, and you want two perfect heterosexual children. And if you're going to have a lover on the side you want him to come when you call and stay out of sight and not make demands."

"No, I . . ." she said, leaning back into her seat, but she felt instantly the truth of his words and was unable to think of a way to argue against them.

"It's hard as hell for me, Donna," he said, this time taking her hand and squeezing it. "Everybody in town, at school, is

184

talking about this thing. Your name comes up all the time, and my heart just crashes around inside me. I want to defend you — even though I don't agree with you — and I want to say you matter to me and we're together, but . . ." He trailed off, shaking his head. "It's just too hard. I need a clean break." He looked at her, and a trill of fear vibrated in her ribs. "Unless you could tell me now that you'd leave him today and we could be married. But I won't settle for anything less. Not anymore. I don't want to grow to hate myself. And I would, because I could never hate you."

She hugged her arms to herself and shut her eyes. She wanted to scream and cry and beg and promise anything — anything so that he would not open the car door and walk out and all they'd be left to do was nod at each other politely at PTO meetings. She saw it all unfurling in front of her, the worst of her lonely imaginings. She had not told him about Hugh's threat to leave. And why not? Because she didn't believe him, not completely, and because it was humiliating. But she toyed with it now, as a kind of half promise she could offer. "Jim, couldn't you be patient just a little while longer? With all that's going on now —"

"That's what I thought," he said, smiling sadly. "Good-bye, Donna." He leaned over and she squeezed her eyes shut tight as she felt the moist warmth of his lips on her cheek. She kept them shut as she heard the car door open and close, and the crunch of the gravel as his car pulled away. She kept them shut as she rested her forehead against the steering wheel and felt her life spinning out of control.

...33

The cafeteria was filled to overflowing by the time Lela arrived. That meant more than three hundred people had turned out. Every chair was taken, and people lined the window ledges and leaned against the tiled walls. For a confused moment, Lela thought she had turned up at the wrong place, because surely this crowd could not have assembled just for her.

Rita was waiting at the side entrance, as planned, so that they could avoid the general public coming through the main doors. "I thought maybe you were going to be a no-show," Rita said, snapping Lela out of her stunned staring. "I've had no-shows before. Had one guy who was never found again. I don't like those. I didn't think you were one of those."

"I can't get over the size of the turn-out," Lela said, her stomach crimping in fear.

"Those flyers did just what they were intended to do," Rita said. She looked somber in her navy knit dress and string of pearls. Suddenly Lela wished she, too, had worn pearls, and something that would have gone with pearls, instead of her olive pants suit. A woman in pearls never looked like a pervert.

"How's the blood lust factor — can you tell?" Lela asked, looking past Rita at the crowd. People were chatting amiably, like an audience before the start of a movie. She tried, without success, to spot Kit and gave in to a little spasm of disappointment. She didn't realize until now how much she needed to see friendly faces; Rita was, after all, obligated by the teachers' union to be here.

"Well, you can never be sure," Rita said. "But mostly the malcontents show up, whatever the issue. Whoever has something to complain about — better equipment, lower taxes, more money for the football team. The people who are happy with the way things are hardly ever turn out to say so. But then," Rita said, "you weren't expecting a fan club."

Lela managed a smile. "I haven't made this easy for you, have I?"

"It's just that, as much as I'd like to, I've got to talk details tonight, not philosophy. I'm not going to be able to argue the wrongheadedness of 6540. The board has the power to adopt these things on their own, without a general vote. And then they answer for their decisions at reelection time. Of course, you can challenge that with the State Board of Ed, if you've got the patience to take it that far. And then maybe the civil courts if you've really got a lot of time on your hands. Speaking of time," she said, looking at her watch, "we'd better get in there."

Lela sucked in her breath and kept her eyes trained on Rita's back. No doubt anticipating the crowd, a riser had been brought in so that the proceedings would be visible to all. As soon as they were seated, a hush came over the cafeteria, and the board members filed in.

Lela watched, recognizing them all: Doug Douglass, Beverly Ferguson, Phil Ferrante — who sat in the middle again, Lisa MacDonald and Jamie Walsh. Jamie had her blond hair up in a prim bun this time and wore a red and gray checked jumper with what looked like, from Lela's vantage, a lapel pin of a mother cradling a child. Lela scanned the front row of the audience and picked out Jim Fallon, leaning forward and rubbing his hands together like a coach before the big game. Farther down the row was Donna Matson and Cathy Reilly. Next to them was Tim Cox, looking as uncomfortable as a zoo animal dressed in a suit and tie, flanked by, she assumed, his parents. A seat over was Ron Banks, preppy in a sweater; the man next to him looked to be his father. Lela gazed over the rows and rows behind them, but the faces blurred into so many bald spots and headbands.

"This hearing will come to order," Phil Ferrante said into the mike with a blast of high-pitched feedback. He thumped the mike several times till it stopped, and then quickly introduced himself and the board, although Lela had the feeling their names were well-known to everyone. "Thank you all for coming tonight. We appreciate your interest in the school and your children's education. Unfortunately —" he said, letting the word hang ominously over the crowd — "we're not here tonight on a happy mission. One of our teachers, Lela Johns, is here for violating the terms of her probation. A month ago, she was admonished to adhere strictly to school policy 6540, which, as many of you know, very clearly disallows teachers from making statements or creating curriculum that encourages or supports homosexuality as a normal or positive lifestyle alternative." A worried murmur rippled through the crowd. "Now, we are not here to retread that hearing," Phil said with a trace of irritation. Lela wondered if he had a card game he wanted to rush off to, or if he actually harbored some sense of decency. "What we were able to establish without dispute was that Lela Johns gave two of her female students the name and phone number of a gay teen support group."

Lela pinched the bridge of her nose as outraged gasps rose from the floor like little geysers. Phil Ferrante was a smooth operator, she realized. He skipped all the stridency of Jamie Walsh's style and managed to appear as though he was a dispassionate imparter of facts. But there was nothing like facts out of context to do serious damage.

"Please, quiet, please," Phil continued. "Tonight we have a charge that Lela Johns disregarded our warning and again violated school board policy 6540. Tim Cox, a student in her class, will report. Tim, please come up."

Lela leaned over and whispered into Rita's ear. "How come we get to hear from the kids this time, but not last time? Because the girls wouldn't have backed up the school board's version of events?"

"That," Rita said, "and the fact that the school board gets to make up the rules as it goes along, basically. This isn't the Supreme Court." Rita sounded as disgusted as Lela felt.

Tim gracelessly pounded up the three steps to the standing mike. He cleared his throat noisily, and for a moment Lela wondered if he might actually spit.

"Tim, please tell us all what happened in your English class on Monday of this week," Phil prompted paternally.

"Well, uh," Tim said, his hands clasped demurely in front of him, "Ms. Johns was late getting to class —" nice touch, Lela thought bitterly — "and, uh, we had all been just talking amongst ourselves waiting for her to show." He swallowed audibly. "And, uh, she came in and said, you know, sounding angry, 'Are you all gossiping about me and the girls who ran off? Because if you are,' she said, 'their being oriented to be lesbians —' " here Lela felt her cheeks burn hot and shook her head — " 'is just fine, and no one can or should try to change them.' "

The audience was roiling now, and Phil shouted them into silence again. "What else, Tim? Then what happened?"

Tim hung his head and scratched the back of his neck.

"It's okay, Tim. You're a brave young man. You're among friends."

Lela thought she might actually get sick.

"Well, um, then me and Ron, Ron Banks, you know, we both said to her that, as far as we knew and were always taught, homosexuality was wrong, and why was she telling us otherwise?"

"Go on, Tim."

"And then," he said, sighing heavily, "she said, 'Guys like you just want to rape girls like Carly and Fran —'" A roar went through the audience, and Tim raised his voice over it. "And if it were up to her, she'd have us arrested for that."

There was such full-blown chaos in the room now that even Phil Ferrante couldn't smooth it over. Parents were on their feet, shouting and punching the air with their fists. It was a mob, and even though they were in what Lela had always considered relatively civilized suburbia, Lela was suddenly afraid for her physical safety. She heard Phil shouting for order, and she knew, dimly, that Rita was clasping her shoulder. At that moment, she spotted Kit in the audience and locked eyes with her across the room.

After several minutes, the crowd quieted enough for Phil to continue, but there was a combustibility in the air that hadn't been there before. "Now, we have to, as best we can, establish the facts," Phil said, sounding weary. "First, Ron Banks, can you please acknowledge if this is all true as you remember it, and if not, come up to the mike to explain."

Ron stood up, soldier straight. "That's the way it happened, sir, like Tim says."

While the crowd was shouting again, Lela whispered harshly to Rita. "This is insane. Where's Melissa McGrath? She knows what was actually said. She led the kids in applause after I cut this clown down to size."

Rita whispered back. "Maybe her parents didn't want her to stick her neck out for you. Besides, we can hardly bring up now that you'd like to call yet another girl student to your defense."

"Jesus," Lela said.

"Rita, your client has the opportunity to defend herself," Phil said.

Rita stood up and scanned the crowd. Lela was relieved to have her speak first. Her own legs had started to quake and she was afraid her voice would be equally shaky.

"Phil, the entire school board, parents and friends of education," Rita began. "Again, as last time, I want the record to show that neither I nor Lela Johns have been given any advance notice of the charges here tonight and have had no time to prepare."

"What's to prepare? Just tell the truth!" came an angry male voice from the audience.

"Everyone will have a turn to speak," Phil boomed into the mike, "and I will not tolerate rude interruptions tonight."

"Thank you," Rita said with painstaking politeness. "It would have been useful to prepare only because what is being said here tonight is a shock, and deeply offensive to me and my client. It is patently untrue, it is offensive, it is a distortion to the point of fabrication, and it is slanderous." Lela listened and felt her spirits lifting. She and Rita had, of course, prepped, because Lela had known that the exchange with Tim and Ron was what she was going to be called on to explain. She just hadn't been able to guess how badly twisted out of shape it would become.

"Since you are calling one of our students a liar, I am certainly eager to hear Lela Johns, who is already on probation, explain herself," Jamie Walsh said. Rita pushed the table mike in Lela's direction.

Lela choked. Sweat dampened the back of her neck. She didn't know where to begin. She stared at the mike as if it were a loaded gun.

Phil, apparently sensing her hesitation, prodded her cautiously. "Ms. Johns, did you tell your class that being a

191

lesbian was just fine and such a person shouldn't try to change her orientation?"

Lela was confused. It was a trick question, she knew, but she couldn't easily find the trap in it. What he said was what she believed. But she knew she couldn't say so. "I have to start from the beginning," Lela said, trying to buy herself time to think clearly. She scanned the audience and saw the hundreds of pairs of eyes boring into her. "An accident had tied up traffic, and when I arrived a few minutes late that morning, the class was caught up in a heated debate about something," she said, hearing the wobble in her voice as it was amplified through the room. "I asked what was going on. I never guessed at the subject, certainly never introduced the subject of lesbianism." She took a deep breath, needing to calm herself from the shock of saying the word out loud. "Tim Cox freely offered that he had been expounding on the fact that, as he put it, 'Any lezzie could be fixed with a good screw, even if she fought it off at first.' " She paused to let this sink in. Tim's mother was holding him by the arm while he jerked in his seat like a balloon in an updraft. "And I told him, for the benefit of the whole class, that sexual orientation was innate and that if he was suggesting fixing it by way of rape, that I was here to remind him that rape was a crime."

"So in fact," Jamie Walsh pounced, "you admit that you accused a Franklin High student — a student from a fine, church-going family who has never a day in his life being in any kind of trouble — of aspiring to be a rapist?"

" 'Fighting off a good screw' was Tim's choice of terminology, Ms. Walsh, and I'd be very interested to hear what you think, in this context, it's a euphemism for," Lela said.

"We can all do without the sarcasm!" Phil said, plainly exasperated.

"It's *Mrs.* Walsh, and maybe, from your perspective, all sexual interest expressed by a male in a female is on par with rape," Jamie barreled on, warming to the attention of the audience.

Lela felt herself getting control her of voice. "To address

just one of your distortions at a time, Tim Cox was not expressing interest in *dating* the girls," Lela said. "And I certainly was not going to stand in front of a class and allow any student to recommend rape as the antidote to anything he happened to find offensive. Secondly, the only perspective I have in my classroom is as a teacher with the best interests of her students in mind."

"Since you cite your respect for your role as a teacher," Jamie Walsh said, "I find it ironic that, in line with Policy 6540, you simply did not tell him that his language was inappropriate and then move on. What is it that possessed you to go so far afield and begin to extol the virtues of choosing one's sexual orientation, and then threaten a student with jail for disagreeing with you?"

"I didn't extol anything, but I was under the impression that the laws of the state were still in effect in our classrooms, and that I couldn't allow rape to be referred to jokingly —"

"But you do acknowledge," Jamie Walsh said, "having told your class that sexual orientation is innate, in direct violation of your probation *and* Policy 6540, which explicitly forbids teachers from making statements that communicate that homosexuality is normal or positive?"

"I didn't think it meant I had to stand by silently while a student advocated violence and bigotry. But maybe I misunderstood. Maybe that *is* what the policy's about."

An angry murmur bubbled through the audience. "I advise you to watch your tone, Ms. Johns, and to stick to the issue," Phil said. "And I believe Mrs. Walsh's point is that in clarifying to your class, *whatever* the prompt, that orientation is innate is to communicate that it is normal. Do you deny that?"

"The context is important, is *my* point," Lela said. "Yes, I said that orientation could not be changed with a good screw."

"And did you think it could be encouraged by urging your students to call gay hotlines that pass out addresses of gay bars? And allowing them to drop by your apartment late at night to discuss their homosexual adventures," Jamie said, "which is what you concede you did back in April?"

The crowd's angry grumble started again.

"Jamie, that's enough now —" Phil attempted.

"I *never* conceded that," Lela shouted. "I told the board I drove home a distraught student who, for months, was too afraid to confide in anyone including her mother —"

"Excuse me!" Donna Matson shot up from her seat. "How *dare* you presume to know what is or was in my daughter's head? The only thing we know for sure is that you drove her home late one night after she was in a gay bar she wouldn't have known about if it were not for you. And the other thing we know is that she has now been missing for almost two weeks!" Lela watched as Donna sagged into the arms of a handsome man beside her and began to cry against his shoulder. Rita squeezed Lela's hand, warning her, Lela surmised, not to get into a public shouting match with a grieving mother. But Lela couldn't stay silent, and she had almost started to speak again when Jim Fallon stood up.

"I'd like to say something," he said. Lisa MacDonald worked the mike free from the stand on stage and passed it down to him. Jim drew in his breath, sending a hissing noise through the room. "I'm Jim Fallon. I'm a teacher here at Franklin High, in the English department, and I share an office with Lela Johns." He turned to smile up at her briefly, a smile she was too surprised to return. "I can't vouch for her private life, any more than she can vouch for mine, and that's the way it should be. All I can tell you is that I've never known her to do a single inappropriate thing with the kids. If she's guilty of anything, it's of inspiring a little too much awe." He looked around the audience before he went on. "I happen to believe that what Lela Johns said in her class this past Monday was right, and I'd have said it myself if faced with the same thing. We cannot, any of us — parents or teachers or school board members — tell our kids that it's okay to hate one group of people even while we tell them

194

it's not okay to hate. We cannot tell our kids that it's fine to rate a human being's worth according to some pecking order we've assigned, even while we tell them that everything about our society — from the law to religion — says that we believe in the inherent equality and worth of all human beings. We cannot tolerate this kind of hypocrisy, least of all in our schools."

"Don't you go and try to tell me what my religion tells me," a woman close to the windows started shouting. "Because the Bible very clearly says that homosexuality is wrong, and it's not normal and it deserves to be punished. And if you want to get technical, the Bible is not opinion, it's fact. But these gays, they choose to be this way, and they are tearing down the family, and they want the rest of us to say they are healthy and have rights, when in fact they are *sick* — sick mentally, and as we know, getting sick physically because of the things they practice sexually. And I for one am sure that we parents are not going to stand by placidly while our school system gives any kind of endorsement to them. That's why I voted for Jamie Walsh, and that's why I'm thrilled about 6540."

"Whatever our feelings about 6540," Phil Ferrante interrupted edgily, "we are not here tonight to reconsider that proposal. I will point out that it was adopted by unanimous vote of this assembled school board. And what's at issue is whether Lela Johns violated it by telling a classful of students that sexual orientation is innate. That is the *only* point here tonight."

"That's right," a man yelled from the back. "I don't pay taxes to send my kids to school so they can be taught gay liberation politics. I send my kids to learn their subjects, and any teacher who veers from that should be thrown out!"

"Hear, hear!" called a band of supporters around him.

"I'm a Franklin High teacher, too," another woman rose to say. "And with all due respect to you, sir," she said, nodding to the man in the back, "being a teacher today is never as simple as sticking to the subjects. Because the kids are human beings, and they come to you with problems, or you see the problems yourself, and if you've got a compassionate bone in your body, you try to help. If I saw a boy standing on the window ledge about to jump because he was told that being homosexual was bad, then by God, I'd tell him it was the best darn thing this side of sunrise — and I don't care what your 6540 policy says!"

"That's different," a large man to her far left stood up to say. "If a kid's life is in danger, you do what you gotta do —"

"Sometimes it's not so crystal clear when a child's life is in danger," came another voice, a voice Lela recognized as Mrs. Sheehan's before she even spotted her, pushing her way out of the aisle and to the front of the room. All eyes watched her making her way up to the mike. "Ten years ago," she said quietly, "my daughter killed herself." Her voice was like a pin in the balloon of hostility that was building, or so Lela imagined. "She was sixteen, and she was in love with another girl. I didn't know that at the time, not really, because my daughter had no one safe to talk to. Me included." Mrs. Sheehan turned to look at the assembled school board members. "I don't know these particular girls involved, and I don't know the parents. But I do know that you can write all the policies you want, and you can fire all the teachers you want, and it won't change a child's heart." Her voice broke and she waited a moment before she went on. "You can't decide a child's life. I learned that too late. You can only decide if you want to be part of it." She put the mike down and headed back for her seat, leaving the audience still and silent.

Jamie Walsh broke the silence. "We're all sorry for your loss, ma'am," she said. Lela hoped she would manage to say something cruel enough to turn the crowd against her. "But with all due respect, the point is that the classroom is not the place to be teaching the homosexual agenda, and the fact that this school board is assembled is proof that parents do not want their teachers to be advocates of the homosexual lifestyle!"

"That's right!" said a woman in the second row, scowling at Lela. "I don't want gays and child molesters teaching my kids!"

"Excuse me, excuse me," came a voice from the right side of the room. "I'm Ann Ellery, with the *Jersey Journal* —" Lela felt her heart leap.

"This hearing is for the parents and teachers of Franklin High, not the press!" Phil shouted.

"Well, this is a public school and a public hearing, and a matter of public interest, sir," Ann said. "So I'm afraid I go with the territory." Lela was surprised but encouraged to hear a tiny smattering of titters, like a faraway wind chime. "What I want to ask the board is, why don't you put 6540 up for a vote from the entire parent-teacher population?"

The crowd broke out into a cacophony of opinion. Phil tapped the microphone testily but was ignored. Lela watched him exchange worried looks with Jamie Walsh, then get up and stand behind her chair to confer.

"This just might have bought you some time," Rita leaned over to whisper. "Those two are pretty cocky, and they might be thinking that if they can win 6540 by popular vote, they could be real heroes to the cause."

Phil went back to his chair, and this time the crowd fell silent without prompting. "The school board unanimously passed Policy 6540, as is its elected right to do so, and I repeat we are not here tonight to reconsider it, but to enforce it. Now, what I've heard is that Lela Johns admits to having violated it, while under probation for the same offense. As such, the board hereby suspends Lela Johns for a week without pay, pending —" here Phil had to raise his voice over a mix of cheers and boos — "our consideration of what further recommendations to make. Can I see a show of hands from the board members in agreement?" Every hand went up. "Our business is finished here tonight, then," he said, rising and leading the small parade of them out the same door they came in.

"What does that mean?" Lela asked Rita as she kept her eye on the crowd and saw Kit making her way toward Ann Ellery, with Mrs. Sheehan at her side.

"Well, it's actually better than I thought. They could have canned you on the spot — and left it to us to take it before the state board. I think they want the week to test the winds and see if the crowd wants your head on a platter."

"What do you think?"

"I think you have a few more friends than you thought," Rita said, standing. "But also a lot more enemies."

Lela felt her gut twist. She always thought she wouldn't care if she lost this job, but that was before. Before she realized she wanted the chance to become the kind of teacher, the kind of person, she and Natalie once deserved to have, and didn't.

...34

After the school board crowd cleared, Lela found Ann Ellery and Kit waiting for her. Ann offered to drive them all to a gay restaurant she knew of about twenty minutes away. They all piled into a big booth in the back where a large, copper-haired waitress brought them coffee on the house. "I've been trying to sweet-talk or guilt-trip this one," she said by way of explanation, winking at Ann, "into a date for a decade."

Lela could see the blush on Ann's narrow face even in the dimly lit booth. She and Kit were sitting across from her. Kit had taken Lela's hand on the glossy wood tabletop.

"Speaking of decades," Ann said, after the waitress had left, "it looks like I'm finally going to get that interview with Mrs. Sheehan. Thanks to you two."

"I don't think we can take the credit," Kit said. "She was clearly just ready. She was unbelievable tonight."

Lela felt a cramp in her chest. "If only Natalie could have seen her . . ." Her vision went blurry with tears and she tried to steel herself against a colossal wave of melancholy.

"You need to prepare yourself, Lela," Ann said. "Because Mrs. Sheehan was the big story tonight, after you, of course. And it's not going to be long before the local press connects the dots between you and her, especially not after my column. People will wonder why she was there, why she traveled from a couple of counties over. A few keyboard entries on Nexis, and bingo, the whole thing's there in black and white."

Lela looked up, rubbing dry her tears. "Are you trying to tell me that you're going to spell it out in your column?"

"No, I won't. At least not the first time. Natalie and her mother deserve their own story. But I can't promise you that I won't report it later. It's my job, no matter how I feel about you — you, too —" she said, taking in Kit, "personally."

"It's my fault," Kit said. "I invited Mrs. Sheehan."

"You invited me, too," Ann said, smiling. "And I guess I'm the real troublemaker."

"No," Lela said. "I'm glad you were there. I was hoping we were going to be able to handle this quietly, but I obviously needed reinforcements. And it looks like I'm going to need to look for another job, if not another profession, no matter what happens."

"What else can I do for you three tonight?" the waitress, smiling coyly, came back to ask.

"Actually, Billie, I think we can use something stronger than coffee," Ann said. "On me."

"If you're still here in an hour," Billie said, "I'm off and can join you. Even up the sides here."

Ann smiled. "One of these days, Billie, I'm going to come to my senses and say yes. But not just yet."

"I hate to still see you with your broken heart on your sleeve, honey," Billie said, turning away with their drink order.

Lela met Ann's eyes for just a second across the table and something electric passed between them; she felt her heart start to pound. She told herself it was just the pull of history between them, the confessions of their last meeting, the sense of shared wounds, the high drama of tonight's proceedings.

"We need the girls to come home," Kit said. Lela was grateful to her for mentioning it, to get her mind off this new problem.

"Since you called me, Kit, I've had my friends in the Bay area on alert, too. One of them is actually a bartender so I have high hopes. She sees every face that comes through there, and she's got a license to be nosy. But there's no guarantee that even if they do come home that that's going to help Lela's case."

"At least it'll diffuse the anxiety of their being missing," Kit said.

"True, but what if they come home with lavender streamers hanging off their foreheads, singing the praises of the lesbian nation? Lela's going to get blamed for that, too."

"Jesus," Lela said. "Would you guys quit talking about me like I'm not here? Besides, I don't think that's going to happen. It's not the tone of the letters Carly's been sending."

Ann's eyes widened, and she leaned forward, lean and intense. "The girl's been *writing* to you?"

Damn, Lela reprimanded herself. She hadn't meant to let that slip. But every time she was in Ann's company, she seemed to let her guard down. "No return address, though, so I have no way to trace or answer her."

Ann leaned back and shook her head, a smile playing around her lips. "Lela, you've got to start telling me things off the record."

"Look, are you a friend, or what?" Lela said, suddenly angry. "I need people around me I can *trust*."

"You're right, I'm sorry," Ann said. "I'm off duty here, the rest of the night."

Billie brought their tray of drinks, and Kit raised her glass in a toast. "Here's to . . ." Lela watched a flood of feelings cross Kit's face. "Here's to," she started again softly, "love." The three of them clicked their glasses solemnly and no one thought of anything to add.

Ann drove them back to the school parking lot, where Kit and Lela had left their cars earlier. Ann honked her good-bye and drove off.

"I want to be with you tonight," Kit said, when Lela walked her to her car.

"I know. But I . . ." Lela trailed off. "I don't know if it's safe." She looked into Kit's face and felt her heart bruise. She had never felt for Kit what had passed across the table tonight between her and Ann. It had been for just a second, but it was enough to remind her that it was possible. She waited, half hoping Kit would do or say something that would make her change her mind.

"Okay, I won't push." Kit smiled and opened her car door. "I'm so proud of you, though," she said.

Lela watched her pull out of the lot before she turned and headed over to her own car. As she put the key in the lock, she saw headlights approaching and whirled, a clawing, animal fear squeezing the air out of her chest.

"Hey, it's just me," came Ann's voice from the open driver's window. She pulled her car alongside Lela's and killed the engine. The moonlight had turned her hair silver. "Come in and talk for a minute?"

Lela felt the roof of her mouth go dry. What was Ann doing back here? She went around to the passenger side and got in.

"I confess I was spying on you from down the road," Ann began a little nervously. "I told myself that if you left with Kit, or followed her car, that I didn't stand a chance. She adores you, that's obvious, and if you feel the same way, stop me now before I say or do something that keeps you from even being my friend."

Lela looked across the empty parking lot. She could pretend not to know what Ann was talking about. But she found she wanted to meet her halfway. "I haven't felt much of anything since Natalie died," she said. "I know that sounds like a long time, but to me, it's just felt like my life. It was a way of getting to keep Natalie, not letting her go. I felt . . . so much like I betrayed her that it seemed like the least I could do, to never love someone else — it was a way to make it up to her for . . . for not dying with her." Lela brushed at the hot tears spilling down her cheeks. "Kit is sweet," she said. "A lot of the women since Natalie were. But no one could get through. But when I met you —" Lela stopped, unpracticed at articulating what was in her heart. "You could be just a mirage. Just some piece of memory, some reminder, some way to revisit the way I used to be able to feel. I'm afraid . . ." She was lost, unable to marshal any more words.

When she looked over, she saw Ann's eyes glistening, too. Ann reached across the seat and took Lela's hand gingerly, as if it were a piece of porcelain. "I'll gladly take that risk," she said, "if you will."

Lela lay awake in Ann's bed. She guessed that it was close to two a.m. Ann was beside her, her eyes closed, her breathing slow. Pluto was curled in a tight ball under the covers at their feet. After they had finished making love, he had padded into the room, all wounded dignity, and claimed what Ann said was his usual place.

Lela was still aroused. It was not because Ann hadn't been energetic — she had. But Lela had grown suddenly greedy. She lay there, aware of her own *aliveness* — of her beating heart, her coursing blood, her power to see and taste and breathe. She seemed miraculous to herself.

"You can't sleep," Ann rolled over to say, her voice silky with affection.

"You aren't sleeping, either," Lela said, feeling a jolt of happiness for Ann's company again.

"You woke me with your thinking."

Lela grinned. All night she'd felt herself rushing toward Ann, propelled on some current. "I'm sorry. I thought I was being quiet."

"You should never aspire to be quiet," Ann said, stroking Lela's thigh with mesmerizing fingers and, when Lela parted her legs welcomingly, entering her, where she was still wet. "Talk to me now," Ann whispered hoarsely as she curled down to take her in her mouth. Lela felt herself being drunk in. She felt her own heat, the melting center of herself being tapped. The coil tightened and tightened and she was high inside its fierce embrace. But Ann was finally too expert, and the coil snapped, and Lela was in a free fall back down to earth.

"Now, what were you thinking?" Ann asked.

"I was thinking exactly this," Lela said. Ann leaned on her side, on one elbow. Lela eyed her frankly, her whippet-thin torso and narrow hips, her surprisingly full breasts. Lela leaned closer and pinched Ann's nipple firmly between her lips. "What are *you* thinking?" Lela asked.

Ann shook her head and rolled on to her back. "Nothing that I should say," she whispered.

Lela nestled closer. "It's you I'm here with, if that's what's worrying you. Not some ghost."

"I just wish it hadn't had to happen to you. I wish you could have been spared the pain of it." Lela could see the glint of tears in Ann's eyes.

In Lela's head, the scene was vivid, as fresh as yesterday: She and Natalie on the walk to the railroad tracks, how absurdly sunny it had been, how maddeningly ordinary the look of the houses and the meadow, how unwavering Natalie had been and how unmoved by Lela's retching and sobbing as she had stumbled along to their execution. How grateful she had been to finally lie down next to Natalie, to kiss the golden hairs at her temple, to hear her words of love, to have her, to *have* her. In her head now, Lela let the train come, she watched it draw near, with all its stupid, deadly power, and she said the words aloud herself this time, "Stay with me, stay with me. Please stay with me."

...35

Dear Ms. Johns:

Just thought I'd check in again and let you know we're still okay.

San Fran is a great city. I think I've decided I want to live here when I graduate from college. I'd even go to college out here but I don't think I could get my mom to go for it.

Fran and I are so in love. I didn't think it could ever be as amazing as this. It's like the colors are deeper, and the music has a melody and, well, I don't want to say more and embarrass myself. But I just __so__ don't understand why people hate us for it. We're not stopping anyone else from loving who they want to love!

I think about you a lot. I hope that's okay. Just knowing that you are part of the world has helped make me brave. And that's why I hate so much to think of what my mom and the school is trying to do. I wish I could call someone and find out what's going on with that. I won't dare call you because Fran put it in my head that they've probably got your phones tapped. But I'm really having a hard time not being there. I feel like I owe you, at the very least, to show up and tell them all that you're a hero, not a demon. But Fran is really not ready to come home.

Her friends took us out to some of the women's bars. It blows my mind! Some of the girls here are so wild, with their crewcuts and their nose rings and their leather vests with nothing on underneath. And my mom thinks she's got her hands full with me!

Love and more,
Carly

P.S. By the time you get this letter, I'll be home. I'm getting on a plane later today. Fran and I had a bad fight. I can't get her to come home with me but I can't stay away from home any longer. My life is there, for now anyway. Well, I'm hoping I can see you soon but I don't know what kind of mess I'm coming home to.

"Oh, my God, where *were* you last night?" Kit said when she opened the door. Her eyes were dark-circled and she was holding a mug of coffee close to her ribs. "I was worried sick! I called you as soon as I got home and kept getting your tape machine." She urged Lela in. "I got dressed and un- dressed twice — I was going to drive straight over to your place and make sure you were okay. But I told myself I couldn't be seen at your place, creeping around in the middle of the night. Lela?" Kit said, taking her by the shoulders. "Are you okay? You look shook up."

Lela shrugged out of her jacket and headed for the couch. When she looked into Kit's face, she lost her nerve. "Carly's home," she said.

"That's great! But how? When? Was she waiting on your doorstep last night? Is that why you weren't home?"

There it was, handed to her on a platter: an alibi that would work. Maybe Kit didn't actually want to know the truth. "No, I got a letter from her this morning that said she'd be home by the time I got it. Fran didn't come with her, though."

Kit waited. "So, where were you last night?"

Lela stood up, rubbed her temple with the heel of her hand. There were no promises between them, Lela knew, but she also knew all along what Kit had been hoping for. "I didn't plan for this to happen, Kit," she said.

Kit looked up at her, clearly puzzled. "For what to happen?"

"I wasn't alone last night," Lela managed.

Kit searched her face. "Ann?"

Lela nodded and held her breath. She looked away when she saw the tears in Kit's eyes. In her head, she'd tried out a million apologies.

"So now what?" Kit whispered.

"I don't know."

"Are you . . . with her?"

"I don't know." Lela folded her arms and shuffled her feet.

"But I don't hear you saying, 'It was just a one-night thing and it doesn't mean anything.' "

Lela bit her bottom lip and looked out the window.

"Well," Kit said. "Well." She rubbed the back of her head. "This is a good one. I've played matchmaker with the woman I wanted for myself."

"I've had a life of bad timing, Kit —"

"No, no, you haven't. You had a genuine tragedy, and it's still claiming victims." Kit stood up. "I'd like you to go. I want to talk more about this, but I can't just now," she said, her voice breaking. "I need time to feel sorry for myself."

It was a kinder exit than she had a right to, and it made Lela wonder if she was doing the right thing. She walked over, stood at Kit's side and gave her a brief, one-armed hug. No, she told herself. It was better this way. Everyone deserved the right to be set free.

...36

"Mom? Mom, it's me. I'm home."

When Donna heard Carly push open the front door and call out, she found herself frozen to the couch. When she had fantasized about this moment, as she had since she got Carly's letter, she had paced out a million different ways she might react. She imagined herself chilly or enraged. The only feeling she hadn't anticipated was the one she was trying to suppress now: sheer, unadulterated joy.

"Mom?" Carly asked, her voice coming closer. Donna held her hand against her mouth to keep from sobbing. When Carly rounded the corner and stepped into the room, Donna finally gave herself over to a spasm of grateful tears. "Mom, Mom, I'm really, really sorry," Carly said, rushing over and putting out her arms.

"You nearly killed me," Donna said, without thought or pretense. It was simply what she felt.

"I'm sorry. I don't want you to be mad at me. I'm so happy to be home. But I needed to get away, to think on my own. I was suffocating. Please don't be mad."

Donna pulled her daughter close. She wouldn't promise anything; she didn't want to think. She wanted just to press her face into Carly's curls, smell her skin, feel her strong back. She wanted this moment to register the fact of her. At her worst moments over the weeks, she had forced herself to imagine what it would be like to live without Carly, if she hadn't come back, ever. And she saw now that it would have been unendurable. She had been imagining pain, but instead it would have been a living, daily death. Oh, that poor, poor woman from the other night, whose daughter had killed herself . . . Donna shivered.

"I'm sorry, Mom,"

"Shhh," Donna said. They had plenty of time to talk. But just now, she had no words.

The three of them sat at the kitchen table, Carly across from her and Hugh. Hugh had been staying close to home, but since his announcement that he was leaving, he had been sleeping in the den. She hadn't let herself think about the future with or without Hugh or Jim; all her emotional reserves had been focused on Carly.

"Carly, your mother and I have a lot we need to discuss with you," Hugh began. "You scared the living daylights out of us, you've screwed up your semester at school, and you've earned yourself a reputation as a flake that's going to take God knows how long to live down. Not to mention this crazy talk all of a sudden about your being a lesbian."

211

Donna felt her stomach buck. She couldn't say she disagreed with Hugh in principle, but she couldn't believe the words he was choosing. If she agreed with him and she was still repelled, what must Carly be feeling? "What we mean, Carly, honey," Donna said, "is that even though we are thanking God you are home safe, you have to face the consequences of your actions. It's your life we're talking about, after all."

Carly looked from one to the other of her parents. "You have to let Ms. Johns keep her job."

"Excuse me?" Hugh said. "What the hell is she talking about?" he asked Donna.

"Carly, this is not the time to discuss Lela Johns. We're talking about *you*."

"That's my point. It's the same thing. Mom, Dad, look, I'm sorry. I know this seems sudden to you, my saying I'm a lesbian. But it isn't. It only feels like that to *you* because I haven't dared say a word about it. But this school policy you're all proud of, that's about me, too. That's what I'm trying to tell you. It says I'm so gross people shouldn't even let the words cross their lips, or if they do, it should be to say I'm no good, I don't deserve to *live*, practically."

"Is this that crazy teacher who's in the papers for being suspended? Is she one of them? Is that's what got you into all this?" Hugh asked.

Donna sagged against the back of her chair and watched Carly give her father a disgusted look. "No, Dad. I figured it out all by myself. But once I did, I needed someone to talk to. And I felt like I could trust Ms. Johns. I don't know anything about what she does in her personal life. And then Mom and her gang decided to trash her." Now Carly turned her disgusted look on Donna.

"Look, Carly, no matter what you say, Lela Johns should not have been giving you gay phone numbers and counseling you on your lesbian love life —"

"She did *what?*" Hugh shouted, slapping the table. "I swear to God, I'll personally break her legs —"

"Will you *stop* being such an *idiot!*" Donna shouted. "Just get out! Get out now, if you're going!" she said, on her feet, hearing her voice rise in octaves. "You don't have any idea about how to be in a family — how to be a companion, a father! So just get out. Get out right now this very minute *now!*"

Hugh and Carly were both looking at her in shocked silence. Hugh pushed away from the table and left the room. Donna waited till she heard the hall closet door open and close, and then the front door.

"Mom, what the hell was that?" Carly asked.

Donna looked up at her daughter and wondered what to say. She hadn't meant for this conversation to come up now. "Your father and I," she began, "haven't been getting along for a while. Somewhere along the way we stopped making each other happy. And I . . ." she said, trailing off. She felt hit with a wave of longing for Jim. He would know what to say right now, what to do.

"You have a right to be happy, Mom. And so do I," Carly said.

"What makes people happy isn't always what's *right*, Carly," Donna said harshly.

"I'm talking about *having* a right, Mom, not *being* right."

"You're just double-talking."

"I want you to save Ms. John's job."

"Well, I can't. Not any more than I could make you come home when I wanted. Anyway, I can't just save her job — even if I wanted to, which I don't."

"If she gets fired, I'm not going back to Franklin," Carly said, her voice shaking. "I'll finish school in California. I don't want a degree from a school run by a bunch of homophobic bigots!"

"Oh, so this is the kind of obscene talk you've learned while you were a runaway."

"What I'm saying isn't obscene, Mom. What you're *doing* is."

"Fine. Go back to California, then! But don't expect me

to pay for it, or to put clothes on your back, or food in your stomach. You can support yourself, then, and see how happy you are. And I won't waste any more of my time worrying about you."

"Fine!" Carly shouted. "I'll go pack and call about flights in the morning." She stomped out of the kitchen, and Donna heard her go up the stairs and slam the door to her room.

Donna got up and looked out the kitchen window into the back yard. The darkness was complete, but Donna imagined she could see the swing set, and Carly on it, sailing back and forth, her hair flying behind her, smiling and laughing. Would that Carly, Donna wondered, ever come home?

...37

Jim Fallon watched Donna make her way toward his booth. The call from her had been a surprise — he had not allowed himself to hope that she would change her mind — and the invitation to meet at the diner near school was even more of a shock. But when she explained that it was about Carly, he tamped down his hopes.

She slid into the seat across from him, barely meeting his eyes. "Jim, thanks so much for coming. I know full well I don't deserve a scrap of courtesy from you."

"Well, I'm here for Carly's sake." He had to be tough; he

refused to be sucked back into some halfway relationship with her.

"I understand," she said, smiling — sadly, he thought. He loved everything about the way she looked: her delicate eyelids, the way her hair curled around her ears, the nearly imperceptible dent at the tip of her nose.

"I heard she's back in one piece," he said. "I'm happy for you both."

"Yes, I was, too, thank you. But the happy reunion was very short-lived. She's hatched a plan to go back to California, to finish school there, unless I can guarantee her that Lela Johns won't lose her job. Because she says she doesn't want a diploma from Franklin as long as it's run by bigots. 'Homophobic bigots' is what she said actually, to quote her correctly."

Jim smiled at the girl's audacity. He admired her plan; as a strategy to pin her mother to the wall, it was actually brilliant. "And what did you say to that?"

The young waiter delivered the pot of tea Jim had ordered — Donna's favorite — and left behind menus.

"What did I *say*?" She looked out the window and pressed her fingers to her temples. "What *could* I say? I said I had no control over it." She looked back at him. "I know I was responsible for getting the ball rolling, Jim. I did what I thought was right. I was hoping you could respect the impulse behind that, even if you didn't agree with the outcome. But now — now it's Jamie Walsh's show. Everybody knows that. Nothing can change her mind."

He poured her tea. She was right. Jamie Walsh was hardly even contrite when that woman from the audience spoke about her daughter killing herself. Jamie's kids were only toddlers. God help them, he thought, when they grew up and suddenly had opinions of their own. "Do you have any ideas? Does Hugh?" The dig was intentional.

"Hugh," she said. "Hugh won't be sharing his opinions anymore. He's moved out. I wish I could tell you it was my suggestion, but it wasn't. In a practical sense, my life hasn't changed much. He was hardly around before anyway."

Jim felt a pressure in his chest, and his next few breaths were hard to draw. This was what he had always wanted to hear, for as long as he'd known Donna. But now that it had happened, she made it sound as if it had nothing to do with him, nothing to do with them. He felt a flash of anger. *Her life hadn't changed much?* How about it had only changed completely? She must have seen the way he was looking at her because her voice softened.

"I was going to tell you — I just . . . not today. I didn't want you to think . . . I mean, it's not like we can do anything about it right now. How would it look? He's not even out of the house a week."

"Jesus Christ, Donna, you're so worried about what other people think of your marriage and your kids — do you even know what you think yourself?"

She pressed her fingertips against the table till they turned white. "Of course I do," she said, spitting out each word. "And I've had nothing but time to think about all of it for the two weeks that Carly was God knows where. But *I* do worry about how what I do affects other people."

"You didn't worry about Lela Johns and ever consider for a second that maybe she acted — or at least thought she was acting — in Carly's best interests."

"Carly ran away because of that woman."

"Maybe Carly ran away because you wouldn't let her talk to that woman."

Donna sighed. "The person I was hoping would talk to her, actually, is you."

He sat back, taken off guard. "You want *me* to talk to Carly? But you know I agree with her more than I agree with you."

"Well, yes, but even so, can't you tell her that this isn't the solution? Running off again. She's not old enough to take care of herself! It's not even legal. I suppose I can have the

217

police drag her back, if they could follow her this time, but I don't think I can live through that again."

Jim rubbed the back of his neck. "Well, I'll do it on one condition."

She fixed him with her full attention. "Tell me."

"I've been in touch with a lawyer. A few of us teachers are going to file suit in federal court, charging that 6540 violates teachers' right of free speech and hurts the kids, too. Don't look so shocked. I've just gotten started. If Lela Johns cuts a deal with the school board, which is what everybody has been guessing will happen, she won't be able to join us. But if Carly sticks around, she can actually help us prepare the arguments by giving the students' perspective."

Donna looked as if she'd been slapped. "You're asking me to sell my soul to save my life."

"Personally, I think it would do your soul good."

She looked down at the table, spreading her hands flat in front of her. "What bothers me more than losing your love, Jim, is losing your respect."

"Who said you lost my love, Donna?" he whispered, his earlobes burning.

"You'll talk to her, then?" she asked.

"I'm sorry I didn't think it of myself."

"I'm not," Donna said. "Because then I wouldn't have had a reason to arrange to see you."

A desperate mother could not be trusted, Jim cautioned himself. But he allowed himself to hope anyway.

...38

Ann opened her apartment door, wiping her hands on the apron she was wearing. Lela handed over the bottle of wine and bouquet she had brought.

"What's all this?" Ann said, pressing the violet and coral flowers to her face and inhaling.

"You mean you don't know? It's our four-day anniversary," Lela said, giving her a sly smile. "Besides, you should talk. I smell another gourmet meal cooking."

"Hardly. Just baby hens and red potatoes. It's the company that counts." She wrapped Lela in a hug, the wine and flowers still in her hands, and kissed her lightly.

Lela felt suddenly shy. They'd spoken on the phone several times a day since their night together, but this was the first time they were seeing each other in person. Lela had been anxious that she might not feel anything but a shadow of what she'd felt that night, but here, in Ann's arms, she saw she needn't have worried.

"We should eat dinner first," Ann said, laughing, and Lela pulled away, embarrassed that her return kisses had turned so hungry so soon. "You're blushing. It's very becoming."

The table was set with candles and two yellow roses, and Ann insisted Lela sit down. "Any mail yet on your column about Mrs. Sheehan?"

"Got the first one today," Ann said, opening the oven door. "From another mother whose child killed himself — a son. With a rifle. She hadn't known he'd been depressed. She said she never found out why he did it, and that's what still made her crazy."

"Hmmm. Hard to say which is worse. Suicide is always a mystery to the survivors, isn't it? Even when you have good clues, the only person who really knows why he or she did it is the one who can't tell you. But I don't want to get heavy on this subject tonight," Lela said, turning her attention to the hen Ann was presenting. "Smells great."

"Right on cue, here's Pluto." The cat sashayed into the kitchen, his tail straight up and twitching. "Hey, boy." Ann put out a bowl of the potatoes and poured Lela's wine for both of them. "I hate to bring this up now, but have you heard from Kit yet?"

Lela shook her head. "She still hasn't returned my calls."

"I feel like such a shit about it."

"I think that's my department."

"Do you think it would be okay if I called her?" Ann said. "To apologize."

"Too weird, I think. If there's such a thing as home-wrecking etiquette, I think the proper thing to do is suffer in silence for a while."

"Oh, thanks!" Ann said. "So you want me to suffer?"

"Never," Lela said. "Never."

"We aren't going to get through my gourmet meal if you keep looking at me like that."

"I just — for the first time in a very long time I'm wondering what the future looks like," Lela said. "I mean, for me, personally. I didn't . . . make plans before. It's thrilling."

Ann put down her fork. "I want this — us — to work, too, Lela. But I worry that I'm taking advantage of you. This is a volatile time for you. And —" she shook her head — "I've been thinking about other things, for starters that I'm nearly twice your age."

"I hadn't noticed," Lela said, smiling.

"Completely unbelievable, but okay, very suave. But then, even more important, what if you don't like cats?"

Lela laughed. "I love cats, I love your cooking, I love the way your brow is all creased up right now. I want to enjoy this."

"But, you know, I still have my job to do. I still have to cover the school board decision. And I'm a little worried that'll come between us somehow."

"It's not like you're going to have the story to yourself," Lela said. "The other local papers will report it, too. And at least I can count on your column for some compassion. At least I think I can."

Ann smiled. "Then what? What will you do if . . . if Franklin does the inevitable?"

"Rita's idea is that we try to negotiate the best behind-the-scenes deal possible. Meaning that the school board gets to say publicly that they kicked me out because of 6540, but my official record will show only that I wasn't hired by the school after a probationary period. Which is bad enough, but at least maybe I could teach again if another school doesn't push for the details. And then we promise Franklin I won't appeal to the state, so their victory isn't threatened. She thinks they'll go for it."

"Interesting," Ann said, resting her chin on her thumb.

"Let me translate. You don't approve."

"Well," Ann said, "it won't do anything to expose and end these policies. But I understand that it allows you to go on with your life. And that *is* more important, no question. I'm not one of these assholes who approves of protests that involve setting yourself on fire."

They cleared the dishes together and gave Pluto a few scraps of hen as a reward for his patience. While the water was running in the sink, and they were brushing past each other scraping dishes and putting away leftovers, Lela allowed herself to imagine what it would be like to live this way, to have a daily life with Ann, to share the mundane as well as the passionate. She found herself grinning.

"What?" Ann said, catching her expression.

"Just happy," Lela said, turning to put her arms around Ann. "I thought I'd forgotten how for good." They stood for a long moment, the water still running, the refrigerator open, the possibilities before them.

June 3, 1996

WHEN SILENCE IS A KIND OF DEATH

By Ann Ellery

Ten years ago, in this same newspaper, I wrote a news report about the death of a teenage girl from St. Ignatius on the railroad tracks right here in town. I wrote that she was sixteen, a promising athlete, a popular student. I wrote that another girl was with her and had fled to safety before the train, unable to stop, carried out its death mission. I wrote that the dead girl's name was Natalie Sheehan, but that the police did not release the other girl's name..

The whole school knew the other girl's name, though: Lela Johns. Almost no one knew that Lela Johns and Natalie Sheehan were secretly in love.

Ten years later, Lela Johns became a teacher at Franklin High in Milltown, and this year she faced another kind of peril. She was threatened with the loss of her job because she told one student it was wrong to commit violence against lesbians, and because she gave another student — who felt strongly she might be a lesbian — the phone number of a support group where she could talk freely.

Lela Johns never once told anyone at her school — not her peers, not her students, not her superiors — that she was a lesbian. She never once brought the subject up on her own in class.

But for ten years Lela Johns suffered because she took on the burden of guilt over Natalie Sheehan's suicide, a suicide exacerbated by the teenager's feelings of isolation, despair and rejection over being a lesbian. If there was no place in the world where Natalie Sheehan could love Lela Johns openly and safely, then there was no place in the world for Natalie Sheehan.

Lela Johns taught at a school where Policy 6540 has been passed unanimously by the school board. It says that any teacher who makes any comment that can be construed to be supportive of homosexuality will be fired. In practice, it also means that teachers must stand by mutely while one student gleefully recommends that lesbians be raped "for their own good," and while another asks for emotional support during a difficult passage to her own sexual self-identity.

A group of Franklin teachers have filed suit in federal court, charging that Policy 6540 violates the First Amendment. What they are fighting for, simply, is the right to go to work every day and not be exempt from the constitutional protections that every other American worker takes for granted.

They are likely to face a long, bruising court battle. That's because social change takes elbow grease. It takes putting a few noses out of joint. It takes maybe having a fight with your neighbor who says things like "God hates fags" while he's doing his edging. And right now it means drumming out of American life anything that sounds even a little bit like Franklin High's Policy 6540.

For Lela John's sake.

For Natalie Sheehan's sake.

Maybe, who knows, for your own kids' sake.

A few of the publications of
THE NAIAD PRESS, INC.
P.O. Box 10543   Tallahassee, Florida 32302
Phone (850) 539-5965
Toll-Free Order Number: 1-800-533-1973
Web Site: WWW.NAIADPRESS.COM
Mail orders welcome. Please include 15% postage.
Write or call for our free catalog which also features an
incredible selection of lesbian videos.

ONE OF OUR OWN by Diane Salvatore. 240 pp. Carly Matson
has a secret. So does Lela Johns.   ISBN 1-56280-243-7 $11.95

DOUBLE TAKEOUT by Tracey Richardson. 176 pp. 3rd Stevie
Houston mystery.   ISBN 1-56280-244-5   11.95

CAPTIVE HEART by Frankie J. Jones. 176 pp. Love in the
fast lane or heartside romance?   ISBN 1-56280-258-5   11.95

WICKED GOOD TIME by Diana Tremain Braund. 224 pp. In
charge at work, out of control in her heart.   ISBN 1-56280-241-0   11.95

SNAKE EYES by Pat Welch. 256 pp. 7th Helen Black mystery.
                        ISBN 1-56280-242-9   11.95

CHANGE OF HEART by Linda Hill. 176 pp. High fashion and
love in a glamorous world.   ISBN 1-56280-238-0   11.95

UNSTRUNG HEART by Robbi Sommers. 176 pp. Putting life
in order again.   ISBN 1-56280-239-9   11.95

BIRDS OF A FEATHER by Jackie Calhoun. 240 pp. Life begins
with love.   ISBN 1-56280-240-2   11.95

THE DRIVE by Trisha Todd. 176 pp. The star of *Claire of the
Moon* tells all!   ISBN 1-56280-237-2   11.95

BOTH SIDES by Saxon Bennett. 240 pp. A community of
women falling in and out of love.   ISBN 1-56280-236-4   11.95

WATERMARK by Karin Kallmaker. 256 pp. One burning
question . . . how to lead her back to love?   ISBN 1-56280-235-6   11.95

THE OTHER WOMAN by Ann O'Leary. 240 pp. Her roguish
way draws women like a magnet.   ISBN 1-56280-234-8   11.95

SILVER THREADS by Lyn Denison.208 pp. Finding her way
back to love . . .   ISBN 1-56280-231-3   11.95

CHIMNEY ROCK BLUES by Janet McClellan. 224 pp. 4th Tru
North mystery.   ISBN 1-56280-233-X   11.95

OMAHA'S BELL by Penny Hayes. 208 pp. Orphaned Keeley Delaney woos the lovely Prudence Morris.   ISBN 1-56280-232-1   11.95

SIXTH SENSE by Kate Calloway. 224 pp. 6th Cassidy James mystery.   ISBN 1-56280-228-3   11.95

DAWN OF THE DANCE by Marianne K. Martin. 224 pp. A dance with an old friend, nothing more . . . yeah!   ISBN 1-56280-229-1   11.95

WEDDING BELL BLUES by Julia Watts. 240 pp. Love, family, and a recipe for success.   ISBN 1-56280-230-5   11.95

THOSE WHO WAIT by Peggy J. Herring. 160 pp. Two sisters . . . in love with the same woman.   ISBN 1-56280-223-2   11.95

WHISPERS IN THE WIND by Frankie J. Jones. 192 pp. "If you don't want this," she whispered, "all you have to say is 'stop.' "   ISBN 1-56280-226-7   11.95

WHEN SOME BODY DISAPPEARS by Therese Szymanski. 192 pp. 3rd Brett Higgins mystery.   ISBN 1-56280-227-5   11.95

THE WAY LIFE SHOULD BE by Diana Braund. 240 pp. Which one will teach her the true meaning of love?   ISBN 1-56280-221-6   11.95

UNTIL THE END by Kaye Davis. 256pp. 3rd Maris Middleton mystery.   ISBN 1-56280-222-4   11.95

FIFTH WHEEL by Kate Calloway. 224 pp. 5th Cassidy James mystery.   ISBN 1-56280-218-6   11.95

JUST YESTERDAY by Linda Hill. 176 pp. Reliving all the passion of yesterday.   ISBN 1-56280-219-4   11.95

THE TOUCH OF YOUR HAND edited by Barbara Grier and Christine Cassidy. 304 pp. Erotic love stories by Naiad Press authors.   ISBN 1-56280-220-8   14.95

WINDROW GARDEN by Janet McClellan. 192 pp. They discover a passion they never dreamed possible.   ISBN 1-56280-216-X   11.95

PAST DUE by Claire McNab. 224 pp. 10th Carol Ashton mystery.   ISBN 1-56280-217-8   11.95

CHRISTABEL by Laura Adams. 224 pp. Two captive hearts and the passion that will set them free.   ISBN 1-56280-214-3   11.95

PRIVATE PASSIONS by Laura DeHart Young. 192 pp. An unforgettable new portrait of lesbian love . . .   ISBN 1-56280-215-1   11.95

BAD MOON RISING by Barbara Johnson. 208 pp. 2nd Colleen Fitzgerald mystery.   ISBN 1-56280-211-9   11.95

RIVER QUAY by Janet McClellan. 208 pp. 3rd Tru North mystery.   ISBN 1-56280-212-7   11.95

ENDLESS LOVE by Lisa Shapiro. 272 pp. To believe, once again, that love can be forever.   ISBN 1-56280-213-5   11.95

FALLEN FROM GRACE by Pat Welch. 256 pp. 6th Helen Black mystery.   ISBN 1-56280-209-7   11.95

THE NAKED EYE by Catherine Ennis. 208 pp. Her lover in the
camera's eye . . .   ISBN 1-56280-210-0   11.95

OVER THE LINE by Tracey Richardson. 176 pp. 2nd Stevie
Houston mystery.   ISBN 1-56280-202-X   11.95

JULIA'S SONG by Ann O'Leary. 208 pp. Strangely
disturbing . . . strangely exciting.   ISBN 1-56280-197-X   11.95

LOVE IN THE BALANCE by Marianne K. Martin. 256 pp.
Weighing the costs of love . . .   ISBN 1-56280-199-6   11.95

PIECE OF MY HEART by Julia Watts. 208 pp. All the
stuff that dreams are made of —   ISBN 1-56280-206-2   11.95

MAKING UP FOR LOST TIME by Karin Kallmaker. 240 pp.
Nobody does it better . . .   ISBN 1-56280-196-1   11.95

GOLD FEVER by Lyn Denison. 224 pp. By author of *Dream
Lover.*   ISBN 1-56280-201-1   11.95

WHEN THE DEAD SPEAK by Therese Szymanski. 224 pp. 2nd
Brett Higgins mystery.   ISBN 1-56280-198-8   11.95

FOURTH DOWN by Kate Calloway. 240 pp. 4th Cassidy James
mystery.   ISBN 1-56280-205-4   11.95

A MOMENT'S INDISCRETION by Peggy J. Herring. 176 pp.
There's a fine line between love and lust . . .   ISBN 1-56280-194-5   11.95

CITY LIGHTS/COUNTRY CANDLES by Penny Hayes. 208 pp.
About the women she has known . . .   ISBN 1-56280-195-3   11.95

POSSESSIONS by Kaye Davis. 240 pp. 2nd Maris Middleton
mystery.   ISBN 1-56280-192-9   11.95

A QUESTION OF LOVE by Saxon Bennett. 208 pp. Every
woman is granted one great love.   ISBN 1-56280-205-4   11.95

RHYTHM TIDE by Frankie J. Jones. 160 pp.   . . . to desire
passionately and be passionately desired.   ISBN 1-56280-189-9   11.95

PENN VALLEY PHOENIX by Janet McClellan. 208 pp. 2nd
Tru North Mystery.   ISBN 1-56280-200-3   11.95

BY RESERVATION ONLY by Jackie Calhoun. 240 pp. A
chance for true happiness.   ISBN 1-56280-191-0   11.95

OLD BLACK MAGIC by Jaye Maiman. 272 pp. 9th Robin
Miller mystery.   ISBN 1-56280-175-9   11.95

LEGACY OF LOVE by Marianne K. Martin. 240 pp. Women
will do anything for her . . .   ISBN 1-56280-184-8   11.95

LETTING GO by Ann O'Leary. 160 pp. Laura, at 39, in love
with 23-year-old Kate.   ISBN 1-56280-183-X   11.95

LADY BE GOOD edited by Barbara Grier and Christine Cassidy.
288 pp. Erotic stories by Naiad Press authors.   ISBN 1-56280-180-5   14.95

CHAIN LETTER by Claire McNab. 288 pp. 9th Carol Ashton
mystery.   ISBN 1-56280-181-3   11.95

NIGHT VISION by Laura Adams. 256 pp. Erotic fantasy romance
by "famous" author.   ISBN 1-56280-182-1   11.95

SEA TO SHINING SEA by Lisa Shapiro. 256 pp. Unable to resist
the raging passion . . .   ISBN 1-56280-177-5   11.95

THIRD DEGREE by Kate Calloway. 224 pp. 3rd Cassidy James
mystery.   ISBN 1-56280-185-6   11.95

WHEN THE DANCING STOPS by Therese Szymanski. 272 pp.
1st Brett Higgins mystery.   ISBN 1-56280-186-4   11.95

PHASES OF THE MOON by Julia Watts. 192 pp. . . . . hungry
for everything life has to offer.   ISBN 1-56280-176-7   11.95

BABY IT'S COLD by Jaye Maiman. 256 pp. 5th Robin Miller
mystery.   ISBN 1-56280-156-2   10.95

CLASS REUNION by Linda Hill. 176 pp. The girl from her
past . . .   ISBN 1-56280-178-3   11.95

DREAM LOVER by Lyn Denison. 224 pp. A soft, sensuous,
romantic fantasy.   ISBN 1-56280-173-1   11.95

FORTY LOVE by Diana Simmonds. 288 pp. Joyous, heart-
warming romance.   ISBN 1-56280-171-6   11.95

IN THE MOOD by Robbi Sommers. 160 pp. The queen of
erotic tension!   ISBN 1-56280-172-4   11.95

SWIMMING CAT COVE by Lauren Douglas. 192 pp. 2nd
Allison O'Neil Mystery.   ISBN 1-56280-168-6   11.95

THE LOVING LESBIAN by Claire McNab and Sharon Gedan.
240 pp. Explore the experiences that make lesbian love unique.
                                                  ISBN 1-56280-169-4   14.95

COURTED by Celia Cohen. 160 pp. Sparkling romantic
encounter.   ISBN 1-56280-166-X   11.95

SEASONS OF THE HEART by Jackie Calhoun. 240 pp. Romance
through the years.   ISBN 1-56280-167-8   11.95

K. C. BOMBER by Janet McClellan. 208 pp. 1st Tru North
mystery.   ISBN 1-56280-157-0   11.95

LAST RITES by Tracey Richardson. 192 pp. 1st Stevie Houston
mystery.   ISBN 1-56280-164-3   11.95

EMBRACE IN MOTION by Karin Kallmaker. 256 pp. A whirlwind
love affair.   ISBN 1-56280-165-1   11.95

HOT CHECK by Peggy J. Herring. 192 pp. Will workaholic Alice
fall for guitarist Ricky?   ISBN 1-56280-163-5   11.95

OLD TIES by Saxon Bennett. 176 pp. Can Cleo surrender to a
passionate new love?   ISBN 1-56280-159-7   11.95

LOVE ON THE LINE by Laura DeHart Young. 176 pp. Will Stef
win Kay's heart?   ISBN 1-56280-162-7   11.95

DEVIL'S LEG CROSSING by Kaye Davis. 192 pp. 1st Maris
Middleton mystery.   ISBN 1-56280-158-9   11.95

COSTA BRAVA by Marta Balletbo Coll. 144 pp. Read the book,
see the movie!   ISBN 1-56280-153-8   11.95

MEETING MAGDALENE & OTHER STORIES by
Marilyn Freeman. 144 pp. Read the book, see the movie!
                                                ISBN 1-56280-170-8   11.95

SECOND FIDDLE by Kate 208 pp. 2nd P.I. Cassidy James
mystery.   ISBN 1-56280-169-6   11.95

LAUREL by Isabel Miller. 128 pp. By the author of the beloved
Patience and Sarah.   ISBN 1-56280-146-5   10.95

LOVE OR MONEY by Jackie Calhoun. 240 pp. The romance of
real life.   ISBN 1-56280-147-3   10.95

SMOKE AND MIRRORS by Pat Welch. 224 pp. 5th Helen Black
Mystery.   ISBN 1-56280-143-0   10.95

DANCING IN THE DARK edited by Barbara Grier & Christine
Cassidy. 272 pp. Erotic love stories by Naiad Press authors.
                                                ISBN 1-56280-144-9   14.95

TIME AND TIME AGAIN by Catherine Ennis. 176 pp. Passionate
love affair.   ISBN 1-56280-145-7   10.95

PAXTON COURT by Diane Salvatore. 256 pp. Erotic and wickedly
funny contemporary tale about the business of learning to live
together.   ISBN 1-56280-114-7   10.95

INNER CIRCLE by Claire McNab. 208 pp. 8th Carol Ashton
Mystery.   ISBN 1-56280-135-X   11.95

LESBIAN SEX: AN ORAL HISTORY by Susan Johnson.
240 pp. Need we say more?   ISBN 1-56280-142-2   14.95

WILD THINGS by Karin Kallmaker. 240 pp. By the undisputed
mistress of lesbian romance.   ISBN 1-56280-139-2   11.95

THE GIRL NEXT DOOR by Mindy Kaplan. 208 pp. Just what
you d expect.   ISBN 1-56280-140-6   11.95

NOW AND THEN by Penny Hayes. 240 pp. Romance on the
westward journey.   ISBN 1-56280-121-X   11.95

HEART ON FIRE by Diana Simmonds. 176 pp. The romantic and
erotic rival of *Curious Wine.*   ISBN 1-56280-152-X   11.95

DEATH AT LAVENDER BAY by Lauren Wright Douglas. 208 pp.
1st Allison O'Neil Mystery.   ISBN 1-56280-085-X   11.95

YES I SAID YES I WILL by Judith McDaniel. 272 pp. Hot
romance by famous author.   ISBN 1-56280-138-4   11.95

FORBIDDEN FIRES by Margaret C. Anderson. Edited by Mathilda
Hills. 176 pp. Famous author's "unpublished" Lesbian romance.
                                                ISBN 1-56280-123-6   21.95

SIDE TRACKS by Teresa Stores. 160 pp. Gender-bending
Lesbians on the road.   ISBN 1-56280-122-8   10.95

WILDWOOD FLOWERS by Julia Watts. 208 pp. Hilarious and
heart-warming tale of true love.   ISBN 1-56280-127-9   10.95

NEVER SAY NEVER by Linda Hill. 224 pp. Rule #1: Never get
involved with . . .   ISBN 1-56280-126-0   11.95

THE WISH LIST by Saxon Bennett. 192 pp. Romance through
the years.   ISBN 1-56280-125-2   10.95

OUT OF THE NIGHT by Kris Bruyer. 192 pp. Spine-tingling
thriller.   ISBN 1-56280-120-1   10.95

LOVE'S HARVEST by Peggy J. Herring. 176 pp. by the author of
Once More With Feeling.   ISBN 1-56280-117-1   10.95

FAMILY SECRETS by Laura DeHart Young. 208 pp. Enthralling
romance and suspense.   ISBN 1-56280-119-8   10.95

INLAND PASSAGE by Jane Rule. 288 pp. Tales exploring conventional & unconventional relationships.   ISBN 0-930044-56-8   10.95

DOUBLE BLUFF by Claire McNab. 208 pp. 7th Carol Ashton
Mystery.   ISBN 1-56280-096-5   10.95

BAR GIRLS by Lauran Hoffman. 176 pp. See the movie, read
the book!   ISBN 1-56280-115-5   10.95

THE FIRST TIME EVER edited by Barbara Grier & Christine
Cassidy. 272 pp. Love stories by Naiad Press authors.
          ISBN 1-56280-086-8   14.95

MISS PETTIBONE AND MISS McGRAW by Brenda Weathers.
208 pp. A charming ghostly love story.   ISBN 1-56280-151-1   10.95

CHANGES by Jackie Calhoun. 208 pp. Involved romance and
relationships.   ISBN 1-56280-083-3   10.95

FAIR PLAY by Rose Beecham. 256 pp. An Amanda Valentine
Mystery.   ISBN 1-56280-081-7   10.95

PAYBACK by Celia Cohen. 176 pp. A gripping thriller of romance,
revenge and betrayal.   ISBN 1-56280-084-1   10.95

THE BEACH AFFAIR by Barbara Johnson. 224 pp. Sizzling
summer romance/mystery/intrigue.   ISBN 1-56280-090-6   10.95

GETTING THERE by Robbi Sommers. 192 pp. Nobody does it
like Robbi!   ISBN 1-56280-099-X   10.95

FINAL CUT by Lisa Haddock. 208 pp. 2nd Carmen Ramirez
Mystery.   ISBN 1-56280-088-4   10.95

FLASHPOINT by Katherine V. Forrest. 256 pp. A Lesbian
blockbuster!   ISBN 1-56280-079-5   10.95

CLAIRE OF THE MOON by Nicole Conn. Audio Book —
Read by Marianne Hyatt.   ISBN 1-56280-113-9   16.95

FOR LOVE AND FOR LIFE: INTIMATE PORTRAITS OF
LESBIAN COUPLES by Susan Johnson. 224 pp.
                              ISBN 1-56280-091-4   14.95

DEVOTION by Mindy Kaplan. 192 pp. See the movie — read
the book!   ISBN 1-56280-093-0   10.95

SOMEONE TO WATCH by Jaye Maiman. 272 pp. 4th Robin
Miller Mystery.   ISBN 1-56280-095-7   10.95

GREENER THAN GRASS by Jennifer Fulton. 208 pp. A young
woman — a stranger in her bed.   ISBN 1-56280-092-2   10.95

TRAVELS WITH DIANA HUNTER by Regine Sands. Erotic
lesbian romp. Audio Book (2 cassettes)   ISBN 1-56280-107-4   16.95

CABIN FEVER by Carol Schmidt. 256 pp. Sizzling suspense
and passion.   ISBN 1-56280-089-1   10.95

THERE WILL BE NO GOODBYES by Laura DeHart Young. 192
pp. Romantic love, strength, and friendship.   ISBN 1-56280-103-1   10.95

FAULTLINE by Sheila Ortiz Taylor. 144 pp. Joyous comic
lesbian novel.   ISBN 1-56280-108-2   9.95

OPEN HOUSE by Pat Welch. 176 pp. 4th Helen Black Mystery.
                             ISBN 1-56280-102-3   10.95

ONCE MORE WITH FEELING by Peggy J. Herring. 240 pp.
Lighthearted, loving romantic adventure.   ISBN 1-56280-089-2   11.95

WHISPERS by Kris Bruyer. 176 pp. Romantic ghost story.
                             ISBN 1-56280-082-5   10.95

NIGHT SONGS by Penny Mickelbury. 224 pp. 2nd Gianna
Maglione Mystery.   ISBN 1-56280-097-3   10.95

GETTING TO THE POINT by Teresa Stores. 256 pp. Classic
southern Lesbian novel.   ISBN 1-56280-100-7   10.95

PAINTED MOON by Karin Kallmaker. 224 pp. Delicious
Kallmaker romance.   ISBN 1-56280-075-2   11.95

THE MYSTERIOUS NAIAD edited by Katherine V. Forrest &
Barbara Grier. 320 pp. Love stories by Naiad Press authors.
                             ISBN 1-56280-074-4   14.95

DAUGHTERS OF A CORAL DAWN by Katherine V. Forrest.
240 pp. Tenth Anniversay Edition.   ISBN 1-56280-104-X   11.95

BODY GUARD by Claire McNab. 208 pp. 6th Carol Ashton
Mystery.   ISBN 1-56280-073-6   11.95

These are just a few of the many Naiad Press titles — we are the oldest and
largest lesbian/feminist publishing company in the world. We also offer an
enormous selection of lesbian video products. Please request a complete
catalog. We offer personal service; we encourage and welcome direct mail
orders from individuals who have limited access to bookstores carrying our
publications.

LOOKING FOR NAIAD?

Buy our books at
www.naiadpress.com

or call our toll-free number
1-800-533-1973

or by fax (24 hours a day)
1-850-539-9731